SAHWIRA

An African Friendship

CAROLYN MARSDEN

AND

PHILIP MERLIN MATZIGKEIT

CANDLEWICK PRESS

First edition 2009

Library of Congress Cataloging-in-Publication Data

Marsden, Carolyn.
Sahwira : an African friendship / Carolyn Marsden and Philip Merlin Matzigkeit —1st ed.
p. cm.
Summary: The strong friendship between two boys, one black and one white, who live on a mission
in Rhodesia, begins to unravel as protests against white colonial rule intensify in 1964.
ISBN 978-0-7636-3575-6
1. Zimbabwe—History—1890–1965—Juvenile fiction.
[1. Zimbabwe—History—1890–1965—Fiction. 2. Best friends—Fiction. 3. Friendship—Fiction.
4. Race relations—Fiction. 5. Blacks—Zimbabwe—Fiction. 6. Missions—Zimbabwe—Fiction.]
I. Matzigkeit, Philip Merlin. II. Title.
PZ7.M35135Sah 2009
[Fic]—dc22 2008028693

2 4 6 8 10 9 7 5 3 1

Printed in the United States of America

This book was typeset in Adobe Caslon.

Candlewick Press
99 Dover Street
Somerville, Massachusetts 02144

visit us at www.candlewick.com

In memory of our fathers
Wesley and Everett Matzigkeit,
two conscientious objectors
C. M. and P. M. M.

For my mother, Ruth Matzigkeit,
and for Bishop Abel Muzorewa,
our Dr. Martin Luther King
P. M. M.

Purple Trumpets

Tucking his thumbs in his pockets like a cowboy, Evan swaggered toward the jacaranda tree blooming with trumpet-shaped flowers.

Cyril, who sat under the tree eating lunch, called out, "Howdy, partner. How ya doin'?"

"Lekker," Evan answered, stepping closer. "I mean, swell." He swatted a mosquito on his forearm, splatting his palm with a drop of blood.

"And what's our Yank up to today?" Cyril asked.

"Roundin' up a few moo-cows." Evan did his best to imitate a Texas drawl.

Cyril laughed, then pretended to swing a lasso toward Evan. "Got ya! Sit down, Cowboy!"

Evan stationed himself upwind of the dreadful yeasty smell of Cyril's Marmite sandwich. The new mosquito bite itched. Before opening his biscuit tin with the picture of the Scottie dog on the outside, he scratched the bite until it reddened.

Cream-colored school buildings enclosed the rectangle of lawn on three sides. The fourth side was open to the rugby and cricket fields. Eating his ham-and-cheese sandwich, Evan gazed beyond the fields to the wild bush of the savanna scrub and the forests of small *msasa* trees. The shrill screech of Christmas beetles filled the yellow air.

An afternoon storm was already brewing, wrapping everything in a damp blanket of heat. In the distance, lightning flashed. Clouds like bruised purple plums crowned the tops of the mountains. Would the rain arrive before lunch break ended?

Leaning down on one elbow, his sandy hair falling across his eyes, Cyril said, "My grandmum sent me a miniature sailboat from England. Maybe you can come over and help me sail it."

"That'd be fun," Evan said. "Maybe after school someday."

But a toy boat was nothing compared with the *real* raft that he and Blessing had found abandoned in the high grass up by the Mission pond. That discovery had occupied his thoughts since last Saturday.

Yet he wouldn't mention the raft to Cyril. It was best to keep school life and Mission life separate.

"Maybe this Saturday," pressed Cyril.

"Maybe." But Evan had already promised Saturday to Blessing. Blessing and the raft.

Johan and Graham sauntered across the grass and plopped themselves down on the carpet of fallen purple flowers. Opening their biscuit tins, they unwrapped more Marmite sandwiches and bit in with gusto.

Evan scooted away, trying not to be obvious. He wished a

breeze would blow away that awful Marmite smell. He lifted a miniature purple trumpet flower from his thermos cup. "Damn! A flower fell in my milk!" He flung it—drops of milk flying—at Johan.

Johan ducked just in time. He took one last bite of his sandwich, then hurled it at Evan.

Evan cried, "Oh, no! A Marmite bomb!"

"The war is on!" Cyril declared. He held a trumpet flower to his lips, making bugle sounds.

Graham picked up another flower and trumpeted along with Cyril. And then, stretching his arms full length, he pretended to hold a real trumpet.

"Here's to our Rhodesian army," said Cyril, lifting his plaid thermos.

Johan joined in with a rat-a-tat drumroll on his sandwich box.

"Rhodies against kaffirs!" yelled Cyril. "Army, army, army!"

"Our army will show those kaffirs not to make trouble!" declared Graham.

Evan shut his biscuit tin. He hated it when the boys talked this way. On the Mission, whites and Africans lived in harmony together.

The storm clouds were rolling in, and the breeze stiffened. Jacaranda flowers fell like purple shadows.

"Without our know-how, those *munts* would starve. And they think they can take it all away from us," said Graham. Because of his Scottish ancestors, every inch of his skin was covered with freckles. Sometimes the boys called him Scottie or Scottie Graham.

Johan suddenly turned to Evan. "I hear your kaffirs in America are troublemakers too."

"Depends on what you call trouble," Evan replied.

"Ha!" said Johan. "It's all trouble." Johan's family came from South Africa. His hair was so blond it was almost white.

"Kaffirs want to take over the world," Graham said.

"Like the Commies," added Cyril.

Johan said, "That Commie Martin Luther Fink is getting the American kaffirs all stirred up."

"It's not *Fink,*" Evan said. "And he's not a Commie."

Evan had watched the riots in newsreels at the movie theater in Umtali. In black and white, he'd seen the clash of Negroes and police in Birmingham, the clubs, the fire hoses, the snarling dogs. He'd seen how bravely the Reverend King was fighting for justice.

"Rain's coming," said Johan. "Run for it!"

The sky broke open, sending everyone dashing for cover.

After school Dad picked Evan up in the plum-colored station wagon, rusty from many rainy seasons. The Africans called it the car that tried to be red.

Dad wore glasses with flesh-colored rims that matched his skin. Whenever Mom was working at the Mission tuckshop, selling warm sodas and tinned meats, Dad picked Evan up.

As Dad pulled out of the circular drive, Evan ran his finger through the dust on the door's armrest, saying, "My friends say mean things about Africans."

"Ignore them. No one knows much at age twelve. Besides"—he glanced over—"you're lucky to have Blessing as a friend. None of them is so lucky."

Evan nodded.

Back in the States, Dad had been a teacher. Here on the Mission, he trained the Africans to teach. Because he spent time around students, Dad always had solutions to school problems.

Dad drove past the plastered houses and neat gardens of the suburbs, then crossed the road leading to Cyril's house. Giant tulip trees edged the road, their leaves a rich, dark green, their flowers fiery orange cups.

Someday soon, Evan would go to Cyril's to sail the little boat. Afterward, they'd take a dip in Cyril's sky-blue pool. Maybe they'd even sleep overnight in the canvas tent.

It would all be fun, but it was the raft, not some toy boat, that made Evan's heart drum with excitement.

The car climbed past the rocky outcropping of the kopje.

It was early in the rainy season, and the *msasa* trees were sprouting deep red and gold leaves. Evan had never seen the leopard that was said to live in the kopje, but every day he stared deep into the forest as the car sped past.

He imagined the leopard moving under the trees, the leafy shadows making irregular splotches over the spotted fur.

Today he saw nothing more than a small brown dassie darting between the granite boulders.

The car continued to crawl up Christmas Pass. At the summit stood a statue of Kingsley Fairbridge, a nineteenth-century white colonialist. The statue depicted Fairbridge at age fourteen, standing tall, gazing off to the horizon as though looking for lands to conquer. His African servant knelt at his feet.

"Today that servant cowers like a loyal dog," Dad always remarked when they passed the statue. "Tomorrow those two will be standing shoulder to shoulder."

The border town of Umtali lay behind them now, nestled in the hills of the Vumba Mountains. Beyond the mountains lay the country of Mozambique, where Evan's family sometimes vacationed at the beach.

Just past the summit, Dad drove by a big green bus. The roof rack was loaded with chickens in baskets and sacks of mealie, the provisions of people headed back to the countryside.

They passed a group of African boys walking along the side of the road, carrying short-handled *mapadza.*

"Hardworking fellows, out of school and off to the fields," Dad said. "Wave to those boys, Evan, and feel lucky that you don't have to dig weeds until dark. Now, when I was a boy in Indiana . . ."

Evan leaned out the window to wave.

The boys waved back.

Dad's voice trailed off before he could describe again how he too had picked vegetables and sold them door-to-door.

Dad slowed the car on the narrow downhill road. In the valley below lay the Mission, the size of a small town.

As the car drew closer, the buildings disappeared into the bluegum trees.

Now crossing the river, where the black bishop birds swooped over the green water, they soon peeled off the gravel highway through the stone pillars marking the Mission gate.

Motoring in, they passed two neat rows of brick African houses, the athletic fields, and the building that housed the printing press—then suddenly, rising out of the blue-gum trees, the steeple of the church, pointing straight to God.

"Remember the visiting pastor who said that heaven was one mile up?" Dad said, smiling.

Evan smiled too and replied, "Closer than going to school."

At last, they entered the area where the white missionaries lived. The corrugated tin roofs were painted red, and the houses had wide *stoeps,* or verandas, on three sides.

As Dad pulled into the driveway and stopped the car, Evan loosened his school tie. "Thanks, Dad," he said, getting out.

"You're most welcome," Dad said.

Evan shut the car door behind him with a thunk. Friday had finally come. Now he wouldn't have to ride anywhere until after he and Blessing had rescued the raft.

The African Queen

Blessing wiped his face with the hem of his shirt. It was panting hot—the sun was at the top of the sky—and they were off to the pond.

He needed distraction from this hot trek, needed to think of anything but walking uphill forever. "Remember the tree house we built in the chinaberry?" he said to Evan, who pushed the empty wheelbarrow. "Remember how we sat way high in the flowers? And they felt so cool. . . ."

"Yeah. Too bad it fell down in the storm," Evan said. "And don't forget the survival pit."

"With the secret door. All those tunnels."

"What about the trampoline we made out of inner tubes and gunnysacks?"

"You fell off. . . ." Blessing recalled the surprised look on Evan's face.

"This raft'll be the best yet."

"Sure thing."

Even if it were not the best, even if Evan were taking him to a pit of hungry lions, Blessing would have gone. He considered Evan his *sahwira,* a friend closer than a brother.

A brother his own age. Because Blessing's own little brother, Caleb, was also close as close to him. Caleb had begged to go fetch the raft, but Blessing had told him no, this would be men's work. Caleb's legs were too short to keep up. He could have a ride when the raft got fixed. Blessing imagined the big smile that would spread across Caleb's face.

With the wheelbarrow squeaking in front, they crossed the dirt dam, the irrigation ditch on one side, the muddy pond on the other. They headed straight for the raft, half buried in the grass.

Evan kicked at the tires lashed to its underside. A rusty wire snapped. A bamboo pole cracked off.

"Maiwe!" Blessing got down in the grass and felt that raft all over—the cracked bamboo, the rotted tires. He looked closer than he had the first time they'd come. That day they'd just been happy. They hadn't cared that the raft was too wrecked to float. Today was different. They were seriously looking the thing over. "It needs work," Blessing said.

"Of course," Evan said, gazing off at the pond.

Blessing looked too. Was that sea of red mud even deep enough to float a raft?

Evan sat down in the little bit of shadow from the wheelbarrow. He patted the ground beside him. "Let's rest."

Blessing got into the shade, sweat pouring off him.

Evan picked blackjack seeds from his socks. "Yeow," he said, throwing a prickly seed, then sucking his finger. His legs above the socks were red with sunburn.

"Serves you right for wearing socks," Blessing said. "Do you even have toes?"

"Yes, ten. But look at you." Evan pointed at Blessing's ankles.

Blessing covered his ankles with his hands. "Blackjacks poking through socks are worse than scratches."

Tossing a blackjack into the air, Evan said, "When the raft is fixed, we'll fish from it."

"And spend the night on it," Blessing added. "We can watch stars."

"We'll spy from it like James Bond."

Blessing closed his eyes and tried to picture the scenes from James Bond's latest movie, *Goldfinger.* Evan had described everything to him in detail because Africans weren't allowed in the whites-only movie theater. In his mind, Blessing saw the tiny airplanes that flew in formation over the gold reserves of a place called Fort Knox.

A spiky red feeling rose in his chest, a feeling not appropriate for a pastor's son. The day Evan had seen *Goldfinger,* he'd gone on and on about it. He'd even taken out the sketchbook he always carried in his back pocket and had drawn scenes from the movie. He'd rubbed it in—the way he'd seen *Goldfinger* and Blessing hadn't.

Now Blessing squeezed his eyes shut even harder. If only he could see those airplanes for himself!

He heard a rustling sound and opened his eyes.

Evan was taking folded sheets of newspaper from his pocket.

"Copy me," he ordered, handing Blessing a piece. He unfolded the newspaper and folded it back into a square.

Soon both pieces of paper were triangles.

"Ta-da," said Evan, opening the triangle and putting it on his head. "An admiral needs a hat."

Blessing put on his hat, tilting it down over his eyes. It gave good shade. Later, he'd show Caleb how to make this hat. And yet he wished that the idea had been his. Evan thought of everything.

On the side of Evan's hat was an ad for skin-lightening cream.

"What're you laughing at?" Evan asked.

Blessing pointed to the ad.

Evan took off the hat, looked, and laughed too.

The other African boys teased Blessing for being best friends with a *bhunu.* Even though he and Evan had been friends since they were Caleb's age, the African boys couldn't get over it. They said that Blessing was after Evan's stuff and the good food at his house.

Blessing did like those things. But they weren't the reason why Evan was his *sahwira.* While the other boys played football, he and Evan played games with a box of postage stamps in the print shop. They collected rocks from streams and hillsides. They built tree forts and trampolines and survival pits.

They loved to play James Bond, pretending they had glasses that could let them see in the dark, capes that made them invisible. They held bananas to their ears, pretending they were using phones disguised as fruit.

The African boys said that Blessing was privileged with a white boy's friendship because he was the pastor's son. They said that wasn't fair, because a pastor's son was already better off than other boys. Blessing's family had more than other families on the Mission. They had real furniture and lived in the biggest house, the pastor's manse. Baba even had a huge American car. According to the African boys, Blessing didn't need a white boy's friendship.

Whenever the boys talked like that, Blessing's head filled with hot blood. He wanted to shout back at them but instead gritted his teeth. He hated what they said and the confusion it triggered.

Baba preached that you were either on Jesus's side or you weren't. If he, Blessing Mudavanhu, entertained hateful thoughts, how could he be good? And if he was bad, how did that fit with being a pastor's son?

But Blessing didn't like to dwell on such thoughts. "Let's get the raft back to your house," he said to Evan.

They stood up and untangled the raft from the grass.

"Here, get this side," Evan said.

They lifted the raft onto the wheelbarrow, but it wobbled off.

"You stay there, and I'll try from here," Evan said. "One, two, three!"

The raft landed on the wheelbarrow and stayed put.

They marched over the dirt dam that formed the pond. Evan went first, walking backward, while Blessing pushed.

Once over the dam, they paused, looking back.

"Do you think the Kariba Dam looks like that?" Blessing gestured at the dam. He hadn't seen the newsreels of Kariba in the whites-only theater. As with *Goldfinger*, Evan had had to tell him everything: how the enormous dam had stopped the river and flooded the valley behind it. How because of Kariba there had to be Operation Noah. Evan had described the way the animals got stunned with dart guns and dragged onto boats, rescued from that flood like in the story of Noah's Ark.

"Kariba is way bigger," Evan answered. "But when we sail, we can pretend it's Lake Kariba."

Blessing wished he'd seen the newsreels for himself so he wouldn't have to ask Evan.

They each took a handle, balancing the wheelbarrow. The steel wheel crushed the rocks on the path.

Salty sweat poured into Blessing's eyes. Bushes brushed against his legs, scratching them, making them itch. Halfway down, he said, "Let's stop there." He motioned with his chin toward the loquat tree.

"Good idea," said Evan.

They pushed the wheelbarrow into the deep shade cast by the stiff green leaves, then climbed onto a low branch.

From here, they could see the whole Mission, spread out like a picture in a book. The steeple of the church poked upward like a sharp white finger. Blessing made out the pastor's manse and, beyond, close to the blue mountains, his family's okra farm, the neat rows shining in the afternoon sun.

Evan took a bite of a round yellow loquat, then spat the seeds onto the path below.

Blessing yanked a loquat from its stem, bit, and spat.

"One of my seeds landed in those thorns," said Evan.

"The wise man planted his in good soil, where it bears fruit. Yours is going to choke. Anyway, mine went farther. Over there, past the little bush," Blessing said. "But let's go. Let's get this over with."

Blessing, then Evan, jumped down from the low branch.

"Look at this." Blessing held out his hands. A blister swelled on each palm. "From pushing."

"I've got 'em too," said Evan. "But what's a bear's fruit?"

Blessing laughed.

They grabbed the splintery wooden handles and moved downhill again. The blisters made Blessing wince every time the wheelbarrow hit a bump. "Baba says if we have faith, we can move mountains. Why can't faith move this wheelbarrow down the hill?"

At the bottom of the hill, the tin plaques appeared. A long time ago, a missionary had put them there to identify the English and Latin names of the trees: golden shower, bottlebrush, *Bambusa vulgaris.*

"Maybe one of these says 'Bear's Fruit,'" Evan said.

The path led into Evan's backyard.

Evan dumped the raft by the door of his *baba*'s toolshed and leaned the wheelbarrow against the wall.

"Finally!" He wiped sweat from his forehead. "Let's get a drink."

Inside the kitchen, the Campbells' house helper, Grace, poured Mazoe Orange Crush into two glasses. She added water and handed Evan and Blessing each a glass.

Blessing drank up quickly—the liquid slippery and cool in his throat—and held out his glass for more.

"Thirsty boy!" Grace said, pouring more of the thick orange syrup. "What kind of mischief have you two been up to?"

"We've rescued a ship," Blessing said.

"A *sheep*?" Grace's eyes widened.

"Not a sheep, a ship," Evan said, teasing Grace about her accent. "But, really, it's just a raft," he said. "Once we get it repaired, we'll take you sailing on the pond."

Grace laughed. "Not me! I don't swim." She put the bottle of Mazoe Orange Crush back in the fridge.

"You won't have to swim, Grace," said Evan. "Our raft will be seaworthy."

This time, Blessing laughed, then sputtered a little when the drink went down the wrong way.

In the toolshed, Mr. Campbell's tools hung on a peg board. Evan handed the pliers, a hammer, and wire cutters down to Blessing, who took them, warm and heavy, into his arms.

Evan climbed onto a stool and dropped down a roll of wire, a bundle of used bicycle inner tubes, and a handful of nails, raising clouds of dust from the toolshed floor.

Outside on the grass, Evan held a brand-new nail over the hole where the old nail had rusted away and fallen out of the bamboo. He raised the hammer and pounded. The rotten bamboo split with a cracking sound.

"Let's try these instead." Blessing wove the inner tubes in and out, tying the tires to the bamboo. "There," he proclaimed. "We don't need nails."

"Pretty good," Evan admitted.

They stood up to look at their work.

"Just like the *Queen Elizabeth,*" joked Evan.

Blessing laughed. "It's not exactly an ocean liner. But let's name it."

"How about the *African Queen*?" said Evan. "I read that book in English class."

"Or *African King*. After the Reverend King."

"That wouldn't work," Evan declared. "That's not how it was in the book. It has to be *Queen*."

Heat bloomed in Blessing's chest. "Okay," he said, to get rid of the feeling. "*Queen*, then."

But secretly, he would go right on calling the raft the *African King*.

The Kingsley Fairbridge Road

On the way to school on Monday, Mom stopped at the tiny Greek-owned grocery to buy the newspaper. Every day there was news of the changes taking place in Rhodesia.

For example, some Africans were now refusing to work for their white bosses.

Some Africans had even *threatened* white people.

And Evan knew from talk on the Mission that young men were leaving their families, heading to the bush for mysterious purposes.

Africans had good reasons to want change. From Mission talk, Evan knew that they couldn't own land in a country that had once been theirs. And, even though they made up the majority of the population, they couldn't vote.

In front of hotels and restaurants, Evan had seen signs posted: EUROPEANS ONLY. Which really meant all white people, Dad had explained, including Americans.

At the post office, Evan and his parents waited in line behind Africans. But some white people cut straight to the front.

And Blessing couldn't go to the movies, which were only for whites. There were no theaters for Africans.

Each morning, when Mom got the newspaper, Evan didn't know what changes to expect. Rhodesia felt like a pot of boiling water about to spill over. Who might get scalded?

He gazed at the gray slatted walls and at Mr. Stanopolis, smoking on the other side of the window.

Finally, Mom came out with the *Umtali Post* tucked under her arm. As she got back in the car, she threw her purse on the seat. She closed her eyes briefly, then unfolded the newspaper with a rustle. "Bad news today, hon. Very bad."

The glaring headlines were blacker, bigger, than Evan had ever seen:

TRAGEDY ON THE
KINGSLEY FAIRBRIDGE ROAD!

He leaned over to make out the smaller print:

Police are investigating a brutal murder. On Sunday evening, a group of Africans, possibly farm laborers, barricaded a country road with sticks and boulders, thus making it impossible for Mr. Petrus Stein to return to his nearby farm. Mr. Stein was then stabbed to death with a bone-handled knife.

Evan felt a sharp pain in his ribs.

"Unfortunately, this tragedy isn't a surprise," said Mom. "It was only a matter of time. . . ."

In the paper, there'd already been several accounts of roadblocks, of white farmers' being waylaid. But there had never been a killing.

Mom spread the newspaper over the steering wheel, taut as a kite. "Not only has Mr. Stein been killed," she said, "but now others will be killed too. While I might sympathize with those men—perhaps they were mistreated—they have done an awful thing."

Finally, she sighed and started the car, saying, "Oh, Evan, honey, this is so sad."

As Mom drove, the newspaper folded neatly on the front seat, Evan wished they were headed back to the Mission instead of to school. At school the boys would be certain the African killers were in the wrong. Automatically, they always took the side of the whites.

On the Mission, people would withhold judgment. They might ask themselves if the white farmer had beaten his laborers. They would wonder if Mr. Stein himself had driven his killers to such an extreme act.

Evan didn't feel like facing the stark certainty of the boys at school.

"We built this bloody country." Graham stood, sweeping his arm as though to take in the whole school, the green lawn steaming in the early-morning heat. "Generations of us hardworking Europeans. And now the bloody *munt*s are trying to drive us out."

This was the kind of talk Evan had expected. He often heard it, but this morning it especially rubbed him the wrong way. "But the Africans were here first . . ." he couldn't help but say. *Scottie Graham,* he said to himself.

"Aww! A kaffir lover," said Graham.

Evan kicked at a tuft of grass.

Johan ran up the narrow path, panting, his white-blond hair flying. "I'm nearly late because my dad had to stop my mum from packing up."

"She'd run away, then?" Graham put his hands on his hips. "Not me. Not our family. We'll stay and fight for what's ours."

"My *mum* was the one afraid. Not me." Johan thrust out his chest.

"Evan here thinks this is the kaffirs' country," said Graham, wrinkling his freckled nose.

"The kaffirs'! My family has been here for three generations," said Johan. "You're the newcomer, Yank. Maybe it's you and your missionaries who shouldn't be meddling here."

The heat rose from the tarmac, mixing together the stench of the toilets and leather satchels.

"You came from somewhere else too," Evan said. He eyed Johan's blond hair, Graham's red mop.

"Rubbish. Our ancestors civilized this place!" Graham shifted his loaded book satchel from one shoulder to the other.

From Cyril, Evan had heard that Graham's grandfather had been a pickpocket in Scotland. He'd heard it was only when he'd gotten off the train in Umtali that he was suddenly ready to civilize others.

"I've heard stories about your granddad," Evan said.

"A bloody pack of lies," Graham retorted.

"Campbell's right," said Johan. "I've heard stories myself."

"Shut your bloody mouths," said Graham.

"What about Josiah?" asked Johan in a low voice, gesturing toward the African groundskeeper, who was wheeling a load of leaves and wilted flowers. "Think he'll try anything?"

"He's too busy working," said Evan.

"He'd better behave," said Graham, lifting his fist. "Tomorrow he might be putting ground glass in our sugar."

Evan watched Dickson, the old janitor, making his way down a corridor with a cart of cleaning supplies. He, along with all Africans, even the completely innocent ones, would be under suspicion now.

The bell clanged, calling the boys to uniform inspection.

His long, thin face drooping, Mr. Young, the art teacher, said, "Lads, the killing of Petrus Stein is terrible. Truly terrible." He tapped a drawing pencil on the edge of the desk. "But remember the distinction between terrs and good Africans. Not every African is a killer. Don't make that mistake, lads. Now set to work."

They'd all done ink drawings, which they'd transferred onto tan, oily-smelling blocks of linoleum. Now the carving would begin.

They took up the curved linoleum knives and set to work. Later, they'd roll ink onto the blocks and stamp the carved images onto paper to make lino prints.

Evan peered at the faint lines on his block: a leopard against a leafy background.

Just as Evan made his first cut, Headmaster Cork strode into the classroom. He paused while everyone stood up, then said, "Be seated, lads."

The boys sat back down, and the headmaster continued. "I want to take this opportunity to offer my condolences to those of you who knew Mr. Stein. He was a fine man."

Mr. Young, even paler than usual, fiddled with a stack of charcoal drawings on his desk.

Mr. Cork stepped into the aisle between the desks. "I want to say to those of you who live on the farms," he continued, "be careful. Be on your guard. But don't panic. Fear has an odor."

Evan ran his fingertip along the side of the sharp blade of his linoleum knife.

Mr. Cork folded his arms across his chest. "Many of you may be going to a funeral," he said.

Everyone grew quiet.

Christian Moore broke the silence. "Mr. Stein was a good bloke. He used to take us swimming."

"And hunting in the bush," added Tom Crowne.

"He will be missed," said Mr. Cork, looking down at the floor.

Mr. Young clasped his hands behind his back and looked down at the floor as well. Again, for a long moment, no one spoke.

At last, Mr. Cork raised his gaze to the ceiling. "Because of the funeral, the rugby game's canceled for Saturday," he said.

One of the boys groaned. The farm boys, sons of men like Mr. Stein, were the best rugby players. There was to have been a Saturday match against Marandellas High School.

"Can't have a game, sorry," Mr. Cork continued, his long mustache drooping. "Timing wouldn't be right."

Evan bit his bottom lip. All day he'd been considering Africans and whites vague groups of people. He hadn't thought of Mr. Stein as a real human being who was now dead.

By the end of the school day, a rainbow hung against tattered remnants of clouds. Water dripped from the roofs and the feathery leaves of the jacarandas. Tiny rivers of red mud ran from the flower beds.

Breaking away from the other boys, Evan headed toward Mom, who waited at the curb in the station wagon.

He saw someone sitting in the front seat. He squinted. *Who had Mom brought with her?* Evan lowered the brim of his hat to shield his eyes from the sun.

Grace!

In the front seat, no less. In his friends' eyes, it wasn't right for Grace to be in the front seat. A white farmer would put his dog in the front rather than an African, and when Evan glanced back, he saw Johan and Cyril, Graham and Adrian, all staring.

Evan's anger swerved toward Grace. Grace knew the rules. She knew she shouldn't be up front.

He thought of opening the front door and ordering her to step out.

Yet when he drew closer, Grace smiled up at him. He saw her smooth brown hands folded neatly in her lap.

With a sigh, Evan opened the back door and threw his school hat onto the seat. How could he have thought to betray Grace, who cooked his meals, who called him Mr. Tomato Sauce and snuck him Mazoe Orange Crush?

As Evan climbed into the backseat, he heard someone say, "Bloody Yankee *kaffir lovers*!"

He got in and shut the car door hard.

"How was your day, hon?" Mom asked, fluffing her curls.

"Awful. I hate this place. I hate those idiots."

Mom pulled out to navigate the circular drive, glancing back in the rearview mirror, questioning him with her eyes.

Mom mustn't ever put Grace in the front seat again. But what could he say? That the boys had called them kaffir lovers? Mom would lower her thick eyebrows: *To avoid a little teasing, you'd humiliate Grace by not letting her sit up front in dignity? You, a missionary boy, would do that?*

ht briefly of how, over his breakfast, he'd let just
n thoughts flit through his mind. He walked
dn't say such a thing. Someone might hear you."
e the side of the Africans?" Evan asked.
ake the side of people who've *killed*?" asked
n unpleasant flutter in his chest. "No one should
'ith the toe of his sandal, Blessing drew a line in
was a line he wouldn't cross. There were things
ntertain, even in the privacy of his own head.
ding to Evan's house, they turned off.
is cardboard suitcase on the *stoep* and followed
pbell's toolshed, at the back of the house. In the
workbench, Blessing found the homemade golf
of hardwood attached to one end, while Evan
tennis balls.
e grass, Blessing knelt over one of the tin cans
backyard, inspecting it. He pulled out a handful
tossing the soggy mess aside, Blessing squeezed
ing leaves oozed out between his fingers.
things inside and outside him he no longer

aying white tennis ball on the grass, lined up, and
nced, then rolled toward the tin can.
club, Blessing tapped the ball. Instead of drop-
fying thud, the ball skirted the hole, wobbling off

"Pure White Sugar"

"It's half past six. Come on. Half past six, getter-uppers, bup-bup-bup-bup-bup . . ." cajoled the voice on the radio.

Blessing reached out, but before he could push the button, a man's voice said, "The news here at the top of the morning concerns a killing on the Kingsley Fairbridge Road." Blessing sat back on his bed, listening. He turned down the volume so Caleb wouldn't hear—he didn't want him to wake up and get scared.

When the commercial for Meikle's Tearoom came on—*"Plumpest raisins in our scones!"*—Blessing turned the radio off and went into the kitchen, where Mai was fixing breakfast. "Someone stabbed a white farmer to death," he announced.

"I know," she said. "Your *baba* got word in the middle of the night. He's in the church office already, preparing his response."

Blessing imagined what Baba would say—that killing, any sort of violence, was the wrong way to solve problems.

He sat down in the straight-backed wooden chair, and Mai brought him a bowl of mealie-meal porridge. He looked into the grainy cereal, then plunged in his spoon. Blessing didn't want to think of the dead white man.

As a small boy, the only white people he'd been aware of had been those on the Mission. He remembered Mrs. Bloomquist holding her pale Swedish fingers tenderly around his, showing him how to hold a pencil.

It was only when he got older that Blessing understood how white people in the larger world kept Africans out of the movies.

Even inside the Mission, things were changing. The older African boys muttered together secretly behind the school. Once, someone had let the air out of the tires on Burly Ford's car.

Blessing had smiled at that. In Mr. Ford's woodworking class, he'd almost finished carving the body of a guitar. Lately he noticed the way Mr. Ford addressed him, saying, "Hey, boy!" as though he were at his beck and call.

Mai brought bread with margarine and a cup of hot, milky tea.

To the tea, Blessing added two spoonfuls of Gold Star, scowling at the words PURE WHITE SUGAR on the box.

After school, Blessing joined the other students in khaki uniforms as they poured out of the blue Mission school building. As he hurried down the concrete steps, he carried a cardboard suitcase filled with books.

The noontime storm had shaken loose the *mupuranga* leaves, scattering them on the wet ground.

"*Mukoma,* Bressin
rolling *r.* "*Unoda kuta*
Blessing shook hi
big old fig tree across
As Wastetime dis
if he should have gon
the bad news, Evan
would harm their frie
But Evan was the
stretched horizontall
deep shade.
"*Maiwe,* such new
"Really horrible."
"That's all everyo
As they set out f
people at your school
"Different things.
"That things will get
have a new excuse to
"Crack down how
"More police Lan
"Didn't some boy
it coming?"
Blessing slowed h
that."
"Why wouldn't y
third-class citizens."

Blessing th
such un-Chri
faster. "You sh
"Don't you
"How can
Blessing. He f
ever be killed."
the dusty road
inappropriate
At the lane
Blessing lai
Evan to Mr. C
gloom beside t
clubs with blo
scrambled for t
Outside on
buried in Evan
of leaves. Befor
so hard the dec
There were
understood.
Evan laid a g
hit. The ball bo
With his ow
ping with a sati
into the grass.

"How Did Your Father Sleep?"

Gripping a pan with oven mitts, heading toward the church, Dad carried roast beef for the Sunday potluck. Grace, her sun hat set firmly on her head, held a pot of potatoes, and Mom balanced stewed tomatoes in a blue bowl.

Evan was glad not to be carrying anything. The air already felt like warm porridge. What awaited him at church this morning? Would all be as usual? Or would the atmosphere feel different, charged somehow, now that a white man had been murdered by Africans?

"Good morning," called out Mr. Deaton, a missionary who helped Dad train the African teachers and drew political cartoons.

He and his wife, Dr. Deaton, who worked in the infirmary, were both redheaded Scots. Evan remembered the way the Africans had once stared at this couple with hair the color of cooked carrots.

Evan wondered if the Deatons also felt on edge this morning.

As he walked under the bright-pink flowers of the bougainvillea-covered arch, Mrs. Makwenga, the leader of Girl Guides, waved.

Smiling with relief, Evan waved back.

After the news spread about the murder, the missionaries had gathered at Burly Ford's house. Evan suspected that they'd discussed the terrible things that had happened to white people—even missionaries—in the liberation uprisings in the Congo and in Kenya.

He imagined that the Africans had also gathered to talk among themselves.

In any case, the following night Blessing's father, the Reverend Mudavanhu, had called together all the adults—missionaries and Africans—for a prayer meeting. No doubt, he'd spoken reassuring words. Had all been healed?

Blessing, wearing his blinding-white Sunday shorts and shirt, ran across the churchyard. "*Mangwanani,* Baba," he said to Dad, panting a little.

"*Mangwanani. Varara here,* Blessing? How did you sleep?" Dad never passed up a chance to practice his Shona.

"I slept well if you slept well."

Dad went on to ask: *How did your father sleep? How did your mother sleep? How did the chickens sleep?*

Blessing's answer was always the same: "*Varara havo kana mararowo.* They slept well if you slept well."

Evan tugged at Blessing's arm, saying, "Let's go."

Inside, the polished red concrete floor reflected the tall windows and the choir, standing in a semicircle. Everyone's skin glistened with sweat. Women fanned themselves with pieces of paper.

Evan followed Blessing to sit in a pew.

Mr. Zezengwe nodded at Evan, and Evan gave him a big nod and a smile in return. Once, when Evan was little and had fallen off his bike, Mr. Zezengwe had helped him up and washed his scrapes.

Evan looked around at the congregation, people familiar now for so many years. There was just a sprinkling of white faces among the African ones.

Evan looked around for his favorite characters. As though nothing unusual had happened, there sat the albino African, nicknamed Tickey, sunburned bright pink, with his stubble of yellow hair. And, sure enough, Baba Sixpence was still wearing a pith helmet and around his neck a brass plaque that read GOD BLESS OUR HAPPY HOME.

Up front sat Mai Sibanda, with her plastic toy rifle. Sometimes she aimed that rifle at those who laughed in church while scolding them soundly.

The missionary dentist from America, Dr. Richardson, sat with a *Reader's Digest* tucked into his hymnal. Evan nudged Blessing and pointed.

In the last pew sat Gladman Chinyanga.

Gladman, a distant cousin of Blessing's, was the leader of the Thursday-night youth group. He gathered his young men at the back of the church. They called themselves the Shumba, or Lions.

Although Gladman was a good Christian, Evan always wished he wasn't seated between him and the door. Gladman had one eye that didn't go in the same direction as the other one. Evan never knew which eye to look at. It was as though Gladman gazed into two different worlds.

As the boarding-school students processed into the church, dressed in their starched whites, the Reverend Mudavanhu began the service with a prayer in Shona.

Evan knew only a few words because Africans spoke the language mostly among themselves. Instead of listening to the service, he took out his pocket sketchbook and fountain pen.

He drew the missionary reading the *Reader's Digest.* He captured the tilt of Dr. Richardson's head, the grip of his hands on the hymnal.

Suddenly, the pen squirted, mucking up Evan's white shirt.

Blessing giggled.

"Shoot," Evan whispered, and, wrapping the pen in his handkerchief, tucked it back in his pocket, along with the sketchbook.

Now that the service was under way, it was time for Blessing's father to begin the sermon. Pews creaked as the missionaries moved to the right of the pulpit, where Mrs. Zezengwe, a tall African woman in a blue cotton frock, awaited them. They'd agreed that sitting in a block together, except when they needed translation, sent the wrong message.

Although Blessing didn't need translation, he always moved up front with Evan.

Evan settled back into the dark wood of the pew. As cloud shapes rose behind the crinkly glass of the windows, the air grew heavier. Evan yawned.

He always found himself watching Blessing's father, who made big, dramatic gestures, rather than the prim Mrs. Zezengwe. He half listened to the reverend's Shona, picking out words here and there.

The Reverend Mudavanhu leaned over the pulpit and cleared his throat.

As the reverend's voice boomed in Shona, Mrs. Zezengwe began her English translation.

"'I must deplore—we must all deplore—the recent killing. Whites and Africans are brothers and sisters in this land of ours. Such violent deeds may bring change. But that change will not be beautiful.'"

Mrs. Zezengwe echoed the reverend's fire with her soft voice.

Evan fanned himself with his sketchbook.

"'The great Hindu leader Mahatma Gandhi, although not a Christian, every month read the Sermon on the Mount, Jesus's sermon on peaceful living. As you all know, Gandhi lived his early life right here in southern Africa. He was later able to liberate the great country of India peacefully.'"

A fly danced along the back of the pew, escaping Mrs. Mudiwa's attempts to swat it with a hymnal. Evan took a swipe with his sketchbook.

The reverend stood tall and raised his arms wide, his satin robes spreading.

Mrs. Zezengwe lifted her arms in imitation.

Evan wished he too could stretch. The pew was so hard, Sunday morning so long!

"'And in America, a great multitude of both Negroes and whites has listened to the Reverend King as he spoke about his dreams for his children, his people, and his nation. He preaches peace. He does not advocate killing white people!'"

The congregation murmured.

"Amen," muttered Blessing.

"Amen," Evan echoed. The pew suddenly didn't feel so hard. He loved hearing about the Reverend King. The Reverend King was straightening out injustices in America. He was setting things straight for people who thought like Johan and Graham. He was America's hope, and maybe the hope of Rhodesia as well.

As they all rose for the final blessing, the reverend raising his arms high, the wind arrived. A cool breeze swept through the open windows, and the whole church darkened. Evan ran his fingers through his damp hair and sighed with relief.

The recessional was played by a slim young man who rocked back and forth in time to the music. *It takes both the black and white keys to make a beautiful melody,* the Reverend Mudavanhu was fond of saying.

Flying Ant

While everyone filed out of the church, Blessing bent down next to Evan as they pretended to straighten the hymnals. By lurking behind, they could be last in the lunch line and not have to be so polite about piling their plates high.

The hymnals smelled moldy, and Blessing held back a sneeze.

"All's clear," whispered Evan.

Blessing followed him out the side door, then down the long hallway that opened onto the courtyard. The wind blew, smelling wet. He held up his hands, letting the coolness tickle the palms.

In the parish hall, he breathed in the good smells of stewed chicken and Mrs. Campbell's roast beef. The potluck was spread on the long tables.

"Here, you two. Get in front of me," called Mrs. Mudiwa.

"No, thank you," Evan called back.

Blessing smiled at her. Mrs. Mudiwa directed the orphanage and was always trying to do nice things for young people.

"There's granadilla pudding," Evan said.

"Yum," Blessing responded. "I love those crunchy seeds!"

Following Evan in the line, Blessing loaded his plate with beef and *sadza, muriwo* and pudding.

When they got through, almost all the seats were taken. Blessing hesitated, looking over the hall, holding his plate with both hands.

Evan nodded toward Burly Ford.

Even though Mr. Ford was helping him make the body of the guitar, Blessing didn't want to sit next to him. Unlike the other missionaries, Mr. Ford might ask Blessing to get him a second helping, as though he were a servant. But there was nowhere else to sit, so Blessing perched on the edge of a nearby chair.

Baba, who'd taken off his church robes, lunched with the Campbells and with a Swedish couple, the Bloomquists. They were both tall and blond. Once they had invited Blessing along with them to Victoria Falls. Across from the Bloomquists, the English Gainsbys sat with plates neatly perched on their laps. Even though Mr. Gainsby had a fake arm with a hook for a hand, he took care of the Mission buildings.

Mrs. Gainsby was heavy and had such tender, white skin, she always wore a hat. She directed the yearly musicals the students performed. Last year it had been *Flower Drum Song,* and this year it would be *Oklahoma!*

Blessing looked up as Gladman and a few of the Shumba carried their plates to the far end of the hall. They too had lurked behind.

Mrs. Zezengwe closed the doors as the rain started with a roar. Silvery sheets of water ran down the windows. Water gushed from the drainpipes. Every time the lightning flashed, everyone got quiet until the thunder rumbled off.

Suddenly, the rain stopped. The windows grew light again, and water ran from the roof in waterfalls.

"Just in time," said Blessing. He gobbled up his granadilla pudding. Then, sure no adult was watching, he licked the bowl.

Evan laughed and licked his bowl too.

Clattering forks and knives, the boys and girls carried their plates to wash them in the sink.

"Don't track that mud back in here," said Mai, holding open the church hall door as everyone went outside. "Mind you don't step in it."

"Yes, Mai," Blessing said. Yet outside, he did what everyone else did—took off his shoes and stuck his feet in the puddles, deep in the delicious red mud.

Faith, Nyasha, and Spiwe ran past Blessing on their way to the court for a game of net ball.

Someone turned on a transistor radio to the sounds of *chimanje manje*—modern, modern—music. Rudo and Gwen danced a jivey little dance, then ran to the mango tree.

Bright, Rishon, and Wastetime were lining up together. Blessing and Evan ran to join that team against Gravy, Kingsize, Petrol, and Lovemore, the largest boys.

"Evan's with me," Blessing said.

Everyone was barefoot except for Gravy, who liked to wear a mucked-up pair of girls' Sunday shoes.

Bottlebrush trees were the goals at one end, chinaberry trees at the other.

Lovemore held up the muddy tennis ball that always served as a football. He kicked off, flipping the ball with his bare toes, sending it high into the air.

Everyone shouted and scrambled, pushed and elbowed.

Blessing dashed around the edge, bumped into Bright, and slipped in the red mud.

Rishon dribbled in and out.

"Here!" Evan shouted, jumping. "Send it to me!"

But Rishon couldn't. Lovemore guarded him, waving his long arms. When Lovemore glanced away, Rishon kicked the ball.

"Go left, Evan!" Blessing called out. Evan wasn't as tough as the others and needed help.

Evan ran left, but Wastetime snagged the ball instead. He sent it to Bright, who bungled it.

Blessing scooted in front of Petrol and knocked the ball back and forth between his ankles, then kicked it to Evan.

Rishon captured it instead.

Kingsize put out a foot and tripped Rishon.

"No fair!" shouted Blessing.

Right then, millions of flying ants hatched. The ground came alive with movement. It seemed as though the soil itself took flight as the ants beat their new wings and lifted into the air.

Abandoning the game, everyone reached to catch the insects. Lovemore put an ant on his tongue and made a show of rubbing his stomach.

Evan stuck his finger in his throat, pretending to throw up. "Bleah!" he shouted.

The boys turned toward Evan.

Blessing stared. What was Evan thinking, acting like that? Everyone loved to eat ants. Why would Evan be so rude? Why would he act like such a *bhunu*?

Kingsize got another ant. "Eat!" He walked toward Evan. "They're good. *Nyama yakanaka!*"

"Bleah!" Evan cried.

Kingsize moved closer.

Rudo and Gwen, who'd been braiding each other's hair under the mango tree, stood up.

Lovemore showed his white teeth and laughed.

Everyone got close to Evan, shouting, "Eat! Eat! Eat!"

Blessing's stomach quivered. The boys had never singled out Evan like this before.

Evan moved back against the wall, calling, "Help, Blessing!"

Blessing ran closer, wondering what he should do.

Kingsize held out the flying ant to Evan. "Eat!" he ordered.

The circle tightened.

"Eat, eat," the boys chanted.

"Don't you like African food?" asked Petrol.

Everyone laughed.

"Help, Blessing!" Evan called again. "They're making me eat the wildlife!"

"Run!" Blessing shouted.

But the boys had pressed too close.

Blessing saw Evan finally open his mouth.

Kingsize placed the ant—wings still trembling—on Evan's tongue. "Now shut your mouth," he ordered, and Evan did so.

Blessing turned away.

"Oh, look, it's Bhunu's friend."

Blessing looked up to find Kingsize towering over him.

"Trying to save that *bhunu,* Pastor's Son?" Petrol asked.

"None of your beeswax," Blessing said. He picked up the tennis ball and hurled it through the goal by the bottlebrush tree.

Serving the Nation

"What was your kaffir girl doing in the front seat of your car last week?" Graham asked at cricket practice.

Evan held the flat bat on one shoulder. Graham's words came at him like an unexpected slap. He glanced at his friend, looking for a smile. Surely Graham was joking.

But Graham wasn't smiling. Johan stood right beside him, his face, too, like that of a carved wooden statue.

"Nothing," Evan muttered. "And don't call her that."

"Call her what?" Graham asked.

"You know," said Evan.

Graham raised his eyebrows and elbowed Johan. "He's got his knickers in a twist," he said.

Johan laughed. "On your mission, do Africans *always* sit in the front seat? Is that customary?"

Graham pressed, "Do some even *drive*?"

"Of course they do," Evan said.

"And what else goes on with those Mission Africans of yours?" asked Johan.

"Nothing." Evan set his feet wider apart. "They're not *my* Africans, anyway."

"Not yours? Then whose?"

Evan swung the bat, testing it. He eyed the green field, his heart knocking against his ribs. He wanted to let them have it. He wanted to speak his mind. After all, he held the bat. If words failed, he could take a swing at these creeps.

"You bloody missionaries. You want the Africans to take over our country, don't you?" said Graham.

"Well?" said Johan.

"Cat got your tongue?" asked Graham. "Those Mission *munt*s been over by Kingsley Fairbridge lately?"

"No more than you have," Evan retorted.

"You're too soft on the kaffirs," said Johan. "You'll change your tune when they start killing you."

"Hey, Campbell!" shouted Robert from the field. "Here comes!" He hurled the red leather ball Evan's way.

Evan stepped forward, sweeping the bat, smacking the ball hard.

While the boys stood and sang a hymn about Christian soldiers marching to war, Headmaster Cork banged out the tune on the piano.

At the end of the hymn, Mr. Cork closed the lid over the piano keys, rose, and bowed his head. "May the eye of God follow us," he intoned, "whenever we diligently walk the path of duty and responsibility."

"Amen," everyone responded.

The dark wooden chairs clattered as the boys sat down. The air was steamy enough to poach an egg, but blazers were mandatory at assembly. Evan loosened his tie.

He looked out the window, to see crows picking through satchels on the green. One pulled out a sandwich and flew off, three others in pursuit, cawing loudly.

When all was quiet, Mr. Cork began, "And now, lads"—he paused, stroking the ends of his mustache—"starting tomorrow, forms three and up will have an opportunity to serve the nation. As of tomorrow, you shall become cadets. This is not optional."

"What's a cadet?" Evan whispered to Cyril.

"A boy soldier," Cyril whispered back.

"Is not," said Graham from behind. "It's a boy *training* to be a soldier."

Mr. Cork banged on the podium. "No need to talk among yourselves. If there are questions, I shall be the one to answer them."

When the headmaster looked elsewhere, Evan pretended to choke himself with his tie, bulging out his eyes.

Robert laughed.

"Every day after school you will train: marching drills, tracking in the forest . . ."

"Tracking what?" Evan couldn't help but whisper.

"Wild animals," Cyril shot back.

Mr. Cork glared in their direction.

Tracking animals sounded like fun. Maybe, Evan thought, he could learn to track the leopard in the kopje.

"Psst, Cowboy," said Cyril, bringing out a Hurricane comic

book. It was filled with drawings of British soldiers chopping through jungle. "Let's skip cadets and join the army."

"Go ahead," said Evan.

Cyril laid the comic book on Evan's lap. "Take it. Just give it back at lunch."

A boy in the front raised his hand. "Will we have cadet uniforms, sir?"

"I was just about to get to that. You may come out now, Johnson."

An older boy, a form-six student, emerged from behind the stage curtain.

A hush fell. Johnson stood at attention in black lace-up boots and tall socks. His belt buckle was of polished brass. His wide-brimmed hat was snapped up on one side. Most impressively, epaulets decorated his shoulders, and medals hung from the pockets of his long-sleeved khaki shirt.

The chairs creaked as the boys strained to look. Johnson seemed so grown up! Evan rose to see over Robert's head, imagining himself all kitted out.

"Johnson looks smart, hey?" Mr. Cork finally said.

Evan nodded, along with everyone else.

On the way home, Mom stopped at the grocery for a loaf of bread and the afternoon paper. As she read, Evan scooted close to read the front page. The lead article told of the police hunt for the Kingsley Fairbridge Road killers. There was a small article about how a white woman's purse had been snatched in Salisbury. Mom pulled her own purse closer.

"No fear. I'm going to be a cadet," Evan said, laying a hand on Mom's small brown purse.

"Is that so?"

"Yes. I'll protect you."

"Hmm," Mom said. "Christians like peace, not fighting."

"But what if someone takes your purse?"

"'Whoever slaps you on your right cheek, turn the other to him also.'"

"So if the thief steals your purse, you'd give him your wedding ring too?" Evan said, staring at the small diamond.

"To avoid violence, I might. You cadets will be expected to rough people up in the name of the nation."

"In cadets we get to track animals. It's just for fun."

"Is it, Evan? My hunch is that you're expected to grow up and fight Africans."

"I'd never fight my friends."

"I'm sure not. But you'd be training to do just that."

Evan stared out the window. School life and Mission life had always been at odds. He wondered if, in spite of what Cork had said, there was a way to avoid joining cadets. Maybe he could help out in the library instead of drilling. Or Mom could write him a note saying that he had an ailment and couldn't participate.

Graham and Johan would spread the word that he was a coward. Or, worse, a traitor to the nation.

When Blessing asked about his school day, Evan wouldn't be able to tell him about cadets.

By the kopje, Mom stopped at the fresh-produce stand under

the shade of a spreading tree. The tree's red flowers pointed skyward like flames.

Mr. Niwatiwa, the proprietor, had a round stomach and plump brown fingers. When he laughed, his cheeks jiggled.

"And how's the little baas today?" Mr. Niwatiwa tucked three guava sweets into Evan's hand.

"Fine, thank you," Evan said. Right away, he popped a sweet into his mouth. The grains of sugar burst with flavor, and his tongue found the bit of jelly.

Mom chose green gem squash, a bag of navy beans, and three purple onions. Mr. Niwatiwa weighed the vegetables and put them in a paper sack.

As they drove away, the car smelled of onion. Evan leaned his head out, taking big gulps of rain-washed air. In spite of what Mom had said, he couldn't help but look forward to the next day's drilling practice. He'd seen movies of soldiers marching together, neat and manly and, most important, moving together like one organism.

That afternoon, Evan helped Dad clean the toolshed. They'd taken down all the tools, had organized them on the bench, and were hanging them back up.

As Dad wiped the hacksaw with an oiled cloth—in such humidity, metal rusted easily—he said, "Your mother told me about the cadet business at school."

"Oh, yeah?" Evan responded. During World War II, Dad had been a conscientious objector, refusing to fight. As a pacifist, Dad wouldn't approve of cadets.

"It concerns me," Dad said, "that the school officials are using you boys for their own purposes. They shouldn't involve you youngsters in adult affairs."

"We're just training, Dad. We're not *fighting* anyone."

"Not yet, anyway. But someone is planning ahead. Someone foresees a long conflict. Hand me that wrench, would you, please?"

Evan held up the red crescent wrench. "It's called an adjustable spanner, Dad. Maybe there won't be a conflict. Maybe things will get solved."

Dad laughed, but not as though he thought anything was funny. "There's already a war going on in the bush."

"A war? Why don't we know about it?"

Dad lowered his voice, saying, "It's all hush-hush. They don't want us to know."

Evan leaned against the workbench, absorbing the news. "Then how do *you* know?"

"Reports come back. Messages are intercepted. Where do you think all the young African men are going?"

"To the bush?"

"That's right. They call it 'gone with the big wind.' Those young men think they're helping themselves and their families. But they're just likely to get killed or locked up." Dad reached for a wood clamp. "We here on the Mission had hoped to help Rhodesia avoid armed conflict. And now your very school is preparing for just that. Making my own son part of it." Dad sighed. "If only there were some other school for you."

"I could go to school with Blessing."

"You'd take away the place of an African boy."

“Looks like I’ll have to be a cadet, then,” Evan said. Dad didn’t know how hard it was for him already, being tugged in two directions. Dad was adding another layer to the load he already bore.

“Your heart will tell you what’s right, son.”

“Being a cadet isn’t optional,” Evan said, knocking at a pair of pliers. They fell off the bench. He felt like kicking them but picked them up instead. “There’s no way out of cadets. I can’t help being one.”

Oklahoma!

At school, Mrs. Gainsby had taught the students all the songs for *Oklahoma!* Now it was time to rehearse the acting in Beit Hall, with its real stage made of concrete.

Blessing ran his fingertips over the red velvet curtains.

People from villages all around would come to see the performances. Blessing would search out Evan's face on the other side of the bright stage lights. Afterward, Mrs. Campbell would bring cupcakes backstage for a cast party.

Lovemore played the ranch hand, Curly. Everyone joked about how he'd have to learn to waltz with Nyasha, who played Laurey, the girl Curly was in love with. Lovemore would get to *love more,* everyone joked.

"Laurey should be played by Tapiwa," said Wastetime. "Then Lovemore will have more to love."

Everyone laughed as hefty Tapiwa walked by.

Petrol was the evil Jud Fry, who was also trying to win the love of Laurey. Blessing had caught him practicing threatening looks in the dressing-room mirror.

Kingsize played Will, who loved the girl who loved the Persian peddler.

In the wings of the theater, the big boys and girls were all trying to kiss and hug. But no one wanted to do those things onstage. And no boy wanted to do anything with Nyasha, who was way too bossy.

Mrs. Gainsby gathered together everyone except the main stars for the scene at the train station.

Caleb and his little friends were singing about corn and elephants while Mrs. Gainsby was trying to organize them into lines for a dance.

Caleb's big ears stuck out from the side of his head. Blessing touched his own ears—did he too look like an elephant?

Blessing waved to Caleb. He put a finger on his lips, signaling that he should listen.

Caleb smiled and quieted.

Tall, blond Mrs. Bloomquist tinkered around on the piano, playing the tune to the dance number at the train station.

Even though they were the stars, the big boys hung out behind the velvet curtain, talking among themselves.

Blessing waited on the other side of the curtain, making sure Caleb paid attention to Mrs. Gainsby.

"*Oklahoma!* is stupid," Petrol was complaining. "All this singing over nothing. *'It's such a swell morning . . .'*" he mimicked in a high falsetto.

"Why do we have to sing about cowboys falling in love?" said Kingsize.

"All this dancing and prancing," Petrol said.

Blessing stepped away from the curtain. He didn't want to hear that kind of talk. He hoped Caleb didn't hear it either. Caleb loved to whistle the songs at home.

Last year no one had complained about *Flower Drum Song*.

Blessing didn't mind *Oklahoma!* The songs had good tunes. But he wished they were doing *Goldfinger* instead.

Suddenly, Petrol yanked the curtain back. "Look who's here."

"It's Blessing, friend of Bhunu," said Kingsize, "listening in."

Petrol strode forward. "He's listening for secrets to tell that missionary boy. Why do you always hang around him?"

"Yeah," said Lovemore, "you act like you worship him."

"You think he's got Jehovah powers?" asked Petrol.

"Evan's fun," he said. "That's all."

"Fun!" shouted Petrol. *"Fun!"*

Blessing dug his fingernails into the palms of his hands.

"You can drink all the Mazoe Orange Crush you want!" shouted Kingsize.

"And you can get *bhunu* Christmas presents and get waited on by African house helpers," said Lovemore.

"Fun!" shouted Petrol. *"Fun!"*

They all three elbowed and shoved one another, while Blessing stared off into the theater, willing his mind to be as dark and still as that black space.

The Drill

"Ten-shun!" Mr. Rollins commanded the next afternoon, his wispy white hair blowing in the breeze. No longer a mere geography teacher, he'd been appointed drillmaster. He was now commander of the green rugby field.

Evan froze, arms stiff at his sides.

"Lads," Mr. Rollins continued, "you are now to call me *Colonel* Rollins. Repeat that!"

"Yes, sir! Colonel Rollins! Yes, sir!" everyone belted out.

"He's not really a colonel, is he?" someone asked behind Evan.

"Back in the old days in India, maybe."

The two boys laughed.

Colonel Rollins pulled his lips tight. "At ease!" he shouted.

Evan relaxed a notch.

"This is how you will salute." Colonel Rollins held his liver-spotted hand above his right eyebrow and snapped it forward.

Evan raised his hand and, on Colonel Rollins's command, saluted along with the others.

"Now, lads," said Colonel Rollins, lifting his knees to demonstrate, "you will march forward. I will clap out the time. Do not make your steps too large."

They began to march.

Colonel Rollins blew his whistle. "Saunders! Are you an elephant?" he shouted. "Smaller steps! Think you're a Jumbo?"

Everyone laughed.

Colonel Rollins walked backward, clapping while the ranks marched toward him, the shoes making a rhythmic thud on the field.

"Quarter turn to the right," Colonel Rollins decreed. He demonstrated. "Then halt and march in place until I give the order to wheel again. Is that clear?"

"Clear as mud," Cyril whispered to Evan.

But Evan didn't feel like joking. Since the killing, it seemed important to move in unison with everyone else. He needed to concentrate.

"Wheel!"

They swished right.

"Halt and march!"

They stamped as Colonel Rollins gave orders three more times.

Colonel Rollins ordered everyone to wheel in a counterclockwise direction and halt. "Very good, lads. At ease."

Adrian raised his hand. "Colonel Rollins, sir. When do we get our cadet uniforms?"

"They're on order. Don't worry. You will all be looking the part in no time."

Adrian hitched his trousers higher around his chubby waist and smiled.

Evan smiled too, imagining putting on that sharp-looking uniform. He'd polish the brass buckle until it reflected every blade of grass on the field.

"Soon, lads, we will be taking a camping trip to the bush. We will celebrate your contribution to the nation."

"Will we stay in tents?" Robert asked.

"Most definitely," said Colonel Rollins.

"And cook out?" asked Adrian.

"That too."

Before Evan could ask if they'd be tracking wild animals, Colonel Rollins said, "Please gather in, lads. I want to show you something. I hope your stomachs are strong."

Evan moved so close that he smelled the spicy pipe smoke clinging to Colonel Rollins's beard.

"This is the work of our brave soldiers in the bush," he said. From his jacket pocket, he pulled a stack of photographs.

As Colonel Rollins turned the top one over, Evan saw an African boy lying in a ditch, his body riddled with bullet holes.

The others were silent. Evan watched as Robert closed his eyes for a long moment before opening them again.

Evan looked at the grass underfoot. That boy lying there could have been Blessing, shot and abandoned.

Yet when Colonel Rollins held up another photograph, and then another, Evan couldn't help but look. Against the background of the cheerful blue sky, Colonel Rollins displayed the black-and-white photos of two more dead Africans—one slumped against a tree, the other thrown over a pile of rocks.

Where had Colonel Rollins gotten these photographs? Was he somehow involved? Who knew about this killing? Evan put a cold hand on his cold forehead.

He wished he hadn't seen the photographs.

"Lads, as you know, we are training for the military. As military, you will be up against ruthless killers. This is how you will deal with those killers, who threaten our nation." Colonel Rollins paused, tucking the photographs back in his pocket. He surveyed the boys standing before him.

Even though Colonel Rollins had put away the photographs, the images floated in Evan's head like bad dreams.

He could never let Blessing know he was training to be a killer of Africans. If Blessing found out, how could they be friends?

Suddenly, even the camping trip didn't sound like fun.

He raised his hand. "Is being a cadet mandatory, sir?"

Colonel Rollins stared. "Either be one or knit socks for your grandmum," he finally said.

Everyone laughed.

Rollins continued to eye Evan.

Evan grew even colder from the look.

"You are dismissed, lads," Colonel Rollins said at last.

As they walked off the field, Graham said, "With soldiers like us, those *munt*s'll never stand a chance."

Evan lagged back.

"How could those *boobijans*, with their sticks and rocks, ever match us?" Johan said. "Oooh, oooh, oooh"—he pretended to be a monkey, scratching his armpits.

The two glanced back at Evan, laughed again, and whispered together.

In geography class, Evan dipped his fountain pen into the inkwell. He flicked open the tiny lever on the pen, sucking up ink.

Colonel Rollins gestured toward the map of Africa that covered the blackboard. "So many of these countries now have different boundaries and even different names." He pointed his long stick with the cone of rubber at the end. "The winds of change are blowing across Africa."

Robert whispered loudly to Cyril, in front of him, "I can smell a wind of change." He pointed to Evan.

"Psst, Yank." Robert turned to Evan. "Change your wind!" He squeezed his nose shut and laughed.

"Poison gas! Breathe it and die!" Evan said.

Colonel Rollins pointed at the pink shape near the bottom of Africa with his stick. "As you know, our nation is no longer *Southern* Rhodesia. We are now simply Rhodesia." He traced the boundaries, then drew an imaginary line under the word *Southern*. "Would someone like to correct our map?"

Everyone raised a hand, including Evan.

"You, Campbell," said Colonel Rollins, tapping the stick on the floor.

Evan marched up and took the black crayon that Colonel Rollins handed him.

As the boys cheered, Evan pressed against the map until it hit the blackboard behind it. Coloring ferociously until the word was hidden under a thick black patch of crayon, he pretended the class was cheering for *him*.

He sat back down.

"Enough of that," said Colonel Rollins. He tugged until the map rolled up with a snap.

Revealed underneath was a poster that Evan had drawn last week of a Shona man in tribal dress. The class had been studying the people of Rhodesia.

But since then someone had changed the poster, drawing big, exaggerated spikes for hair. That someone had drawn a bubble above the head and had written: "I want In-*dep*-a-dense!"

Someone had also drawn another figure on the chalkboard. A stick figure that was obviously white. The bubble above his head read, "No problem, baas." Evan noticed a tiny American flag drawn beside the figure. Was that figure meant to be *him*?

Everyone laughed. Even Colonel Rollins chuckled as he erased the stick figure. Cyril laughed the hardest, red in the face, doubled over.

"Go to hell," Evan muttered, running his fingertip over an ancient set of initials carved in the wooden desk.

Just months ago, when fire had roared into the bush near the school, he and these boys had beaten back the flames with wet *msasa* branches. On and on they'd fought through the scorching afternoon, until the fire had wandered back over the ridge.

And now? If a fire came now, would they fight it together?

This Space Left Blank

"You're just in time, boys," said Mr. Njopera as first Blessing, then Evan, stepped into the room with the printing press. "I'm finishing the last copies."

The newspaper came out every week and was full of news such as who had gotten married, news from churches overseas, inspirational articles by Baba.

Blessing slipped a printer's apron over his neck, tied it at his waist.

Mr. Njopera's bald head shone with sweat as he turned the handle of the printing press.

Blessing's cousin Gladman, who was training with Mr. Njopera as an apprentice, folded pieces of light-yellow paper. He used polished bone to make the fold neat.

On the Supersonic shortwave radio, the voice of the BBC broadcaster sounded far away: "President Johnson affirms continued military support for South Vietnam. . . . And in news of Rhodesia—"

Suddenly, there was only static.

"Ah, they've jammed the station again," said Mr. Njopera, turning off the radio.

He let go of the string that ran around the tray holding the letters in place. He'd been setting each letter by hand. "Go ahead, boys, put them away."

After each newspaper page had been printed, it was Blessing and Evan's job to sort the letters and spacers.

"I'll do all the *A*s," Blessing said, "and you start with the consonants."

As they worked, the letters clunked into their wooden boxes. The tunes to the *Oklahoma!* songs ran through Blessing's head. The smell of grass came in through the open window, along with the odors of cattle, the irrigation ditch, and the latrine.

Gladman whistled as he folded.

A car pulled up outside, and the motor died with a sputter.

Mr. Njopera threw his jacket over the radio.

A moment later, a man with a close-cut gray beard stood in the doorway. The man had come to the printing press before, and Blessing now recognized him as Mr. Furber, the government censor.

Mr. Furber had always been polite, but Blessing wished he wouldn't stand in the doorway, casting his shadow across the room.

Mr. Njopera handed over a copy of the newspaper. "Have a seat, sir," he said.

Mr. Furber climbed onto the stool. He took off his glasses and brought out another pair from his pocket.

As Mr. Furber flipped through the pages of the newspaper,

Blessing and Evan kept sorting, but more slowly. Blessing threw the letter *R* into the *S* box by accident.

Gladman still folded but didn't whistle.

Mr. Furber cleared his throat. He put a fingertip on one of Mr. Deaton's political cartoons. The drawing showed Rhodesian Prime Minister Ian Smith dressed as an oppressive British redcoat and an African dressed as revolutionary George Washington.

Mr. Furber reached into his pocket and took out a small case. He clicked it open and removed a pair of fingernail scissors.

Blessing held his breath. Around him, Evan, Gladman, and Mr. Njopera froze like statues.

Mr. Furber cut out the political cartoon, the scissors clicking. He tucked the scrap of paper in his pocket, then put the scissors back in the case.

Mr. Njopera looked at the floor.

Gladman moved the stack of yellow paper to the paper cutter to trim the edges.

Blessing stopped putting the letters in their boxes. His hands felt heavy, like damp clay. So much work done for nothing.

Mr. Furber paced back and forth, ruffling through papers on the shelves, bending down to look under the furniture. He lifted Mr. Njopera's jacket off the radio, then put it back down.

Blessing looked at Evan and then away. He stared at his fingers, covered with ink. He didn't like Mr. Furber's searching, the implication that there had been something suspicious going on.

Finally, Mr. Furber brushed his hands together. "In light of the recent killing, sir," he said to Mr. Njopera, "it will be wise to err on the side of caution."

"Yes, sir," said Mr. Njopera.

Blessing stood behind Mr. Njopera, watching Mr. Furber get into his car. He felt shamed, yet what had he done?

Mr. Furber took off, leaving a cloud of red dust behind him.

Mr. Njopera sighed. "We'll have to reprint," he said. "You boys can help Gladman and me reset the type."

"That stinks," said Evan.

"The paper can't come out on time now," Blessing said.

Mr. Njopera balanced the el in the crook of his elbow. It was a printer's tool shaped like the letter *L*, and it held the letters.

Blessing and Evan handed him the letters he called for.

From the el, Gladman moved the letters to the large tray.

Blessing concentrated on sorting, trying not to think of Mr. Furber, trying not to dislike him.

It was way past dinnertime when the newspaper was whole again. But it wasn't whole: on page 3 an empty spot read,

THIS SPACE LEFT BLANK

DUE TO GOVERNMENT CENSORSHIP.

Peacock Blue

In Colonel Rollins's geography class, Evan was drawing a map of Rhodesia. He'd almost finished sketching in the Zambezi and its plunge over Victoria Falls, when he looked out the window to see a lorry pull up outside the assembly hall.

Two soldiers unloaded khaki-colored bales.

"Are those our cadet uniforms?" Adrian whispered loudly.

"Looks like it," said Cyril.

Robert poked Adrian in the back. "Hope they have your size. Your shoes are as big as cricket bats."

"Shut your bloody mouth," said Adrian.

"What's going on back there?" Colonel Rollins asked.

Evan watched the men unload the lorry. In some ways, it would be easy to wear the cadet uniform, to look just like the others. He desperately needed to fit in. But whenever he wore that uniform, he'd feel like a hypocrite.

Dad had said that his heart would tell him what to do. But what if his heart's advice was impossible to follow?

As class was about to end, an African messenger appeared in the classroom doorway. The man handed a note to Colonel Rollins.

Colonel Rollins scanned the paper, then cleared his throat. "Lads! You're to be kitted out for cadets. Line up! Bredenkamp, lead everyone to assembly."

Evan added a few more wavy lines to Victoria Falls.

"Let's go, Campbell," Colonel Rollins barked. "Lads, we will march to our destination." When everyone was in line, he blew his whistle.

The boys came to attention.

Colonel Rollins blew the whistle again, and they set off.

Evan kept his footsteps in sync with everyone else's, while his mind tumbled elsewhere. How could he wear the uniform outwardly but inside stay true to himself?

Soldiers, their medals shining, sat behind the tables set up in the assembly hall. The various parts of the uniform were piled high, and the room smelled of new fabric.

Colonel Rollins spoke into a megaphone: "At the end of the year, you will return these uniforms, lads. You must sign for each item. A through C, stand in this line to get hats. D through F, here for boots . . ." He pointed with his rubber-tipped stick.

As Evan got into each line, his friends—busy slapping at each other with shoelaces and belts—wouldn't talk to him or even look at him. They pretended that he wasn't there.

Evan's arms were soon piled high with a belt, a hat, boots, tall socks, a shirt with epaulets, and khaki shorts. Each item locked him deeper into cadets. Each time he needed to sign, he wrote *Evan Campbell* in his most illegible handwriting, feeling like a traitor.

At the final table, each boy was handed a compass. The silver case hinged open and hung by a leather strap around the neck.

Evan slung the compass around his neck right away and sighed at the comforting weight of it. Now, *this* was something he could accept without conflict. He wished life could be as simple as a compass: *This way north. Head in this direction.*

Because the chairs had been moved aside, the boys sat on the floor, the uniforms in their laps. Robert and Adrian, Graham and Johan, and even Cyril gathered in a group conspicuously apart from Evan, flipping their compass cases open and shut.

Evan pretended not to care. He examined the tiny black boat etched underneath the spinning needle. He imagined using the compass to sail the raft.

Evan took out his sketchbook and did a quick drawing of the black boat.

"Silence, lads!" Colonel Rollins said into the megaphone. When the room quieted, he began: "As you know, this country was in a primitive state when the first Europeans arrived. We settlers brought roads and hospitals, schools and bridges. This nation would be a pitiful spot without us."

Evan had heard this kind of talk before. He noticed Cyril nodding, his eyes fixed on Rollins. Outside, two crows shot into the sky.

Colonel Rollins paced. "But now these terrorists would destroy the way of life we've built. In the name of liberation, they would return the country to its undeveloped state. They would drive us from our very homes." He stopped pacing and faced the room head-on. "As I speak, Communist terrorists are massed on the border of Mozambique, preparing their assaults."

The boys murmured. A tingle ran up Evan's spine as Colonel Rollins pinned Evan's eyes with his.

"The terrorists say they only want majority rule," Rollins continued. "That sounds innocent enough. Someday the Africans may be ready for that. But in reality, these terrorists seek something far more sinister. We have proof that they are backed by the totalitarian dictatorships of Communist Russia and China."

Johan and Graham looked at each other, eyes wide. Cyril fiddled with his compass.

"As you know, lads, Communism is a terrible threat to the free world. The people in Communist countries are slaves, completely deprived of freedom. Our nation of Rhodesia is being overrun by Communists. Here is our proof." Colonel Rollins unfolded a piece of peacock-blue paper. He held up a handbill, turning it slowly, showing it first to one side of the room, then the other.

Inked onto the paper was a silhouette of an African soldier, an AK-47 slung across his chest.

"We've got Communist troublemakers on our hands." Colonel Rollins pointed to the word *chimurenga,* which was written above the soldier. "This word is Shona for 'Communism.'"

Evan knew that Colonel Rollins was wrong about that definition. The *chimurenga* was the liberation war. But he *had* heard that

Communism was a powerful force that knocked over whole countries like dominoes. Communists didn't even believe in God.

The image on the handbill was so menacing that Evan shivered. Africans weren't allowed to own guns at all, and here was one kitted out like a soldier and holding a gun right out in the open!

"This, lads, is a likely portrait of one of the killers the police are searching for."

Evan strained to see the details of the handbill. Did this mean that the African killers were *Communists*? If so, that cast a different light on things. He hadn't taken Communism into account when he'd thought matters through. Maybe in America, things were clear-cut between Negroes and whites. But here in Rhodesia, it seemed that there was another force at work. The picture wasn't so simple. Perhaps, after all, the killing hadn't been a simple matter of Africans taking revenge for injustice. What if the murder had been the work of evil Commies?

Evan suddenly remembered the way the African boys had made him eat the flying ant. The peppery taste. The microscopic beat of the wings against his cheek.

"This"—Colonel Rollins rattled the handbill—"is the reason we have organized the cadets here at school. The nation needs to be prepared for the future. And right now, the nation needs your help in capturing terrorists."

Evan sat taller.

Colonel Rollins looked over the group as though sizing each of them up. "The medals you saw on Johnson's pockets are to be earned through acts of bravery. As cadets, you can be the eyes and ears of law and order. If you find out anything useful to the nation, you can bring honor to yourself and to the cadets." He paused, then continued: "You can earn a medal. You can be a hero."

A chill rippled down the back of Evan's neck. *A hero.* That was an idea he hadn't thought of before.

Warm Coca-Cola

Blessing stared at his upside-down reflection in the spoon. "Look, Caleb," he said, showing Caleb his own cockeyed face.

Caleb giggled and grabbed for the spoon, bringing it close, moving it back.

Mai carried the *sadza* and stewed chicken to the table.

Gladman's uncle, Mr. Chinyanga, had come to dinner. Mr. Chinyanga had a long, thin face, with lines crisscrossing his forehead. He leaned on the table, and it rocked toward him.

Blessing bent down to find the cardboard that went under the short leg, but it was missing.

Steam rose from the food, along with the good smells of maize and the tomatoes cooked with the chicken. The chairs just fit around the table.

The room got quiet as everyone ate, while Mai and Blessing's grandmother—his *mbuya*—looked in to make sure people had enough.

Baba passed the dishes, and Caleb started right away on a chicken leg.

Blessing drank up his whole glass of warm Coca-Cola. Soda was a special treat that Mai served only when guests visited.

When Mr. Chinyanga's plate was scraped clean, he pushed himself back a little from the table and said, "My brother used to drive a delivery truck. He was organizing a union of truck drivers. One night, the police took my brother in for questioning. That was months ago. He has never been charged with a crime. But he is still in prison."

"I'm sorry to hear the bad news," said Baba. "It must be hard for the family to have the father away."

That would be Gladman's father, Blessing noted. He tilted up his glass to drain the last drops of Coca-Cola.

"Very hard. That night it took three police to drag my brother off. He was screaming. The whole family was screaming. The children ran after the police Land Rover."

Caleb's eyes got big, and he stopped chewing.

Blessing wondered if Caleb should hear this kind of talk.

Baba closed his eyes for a second.

"And now, every day, every night, every minute, they wait for him to come home." Mr. Chinyanga took a drink of Coca-Cola.

Mai and Mbuya peeked in from the kitchen. Mbuya caught Blessing's eye.

He looked back but didn't smile. Serious stuff was going on here.

Mr. Chinyanga looked around as if there might be spies, then whispered, "Many are taken from the villages. Some return. Many do not."

"I've heard these terrible stories," Baba said. "Now, since the killing, everything will get worse."

"There's already a war going on, Reverend. White Rhodesian soldiers are fighting in the bush. They're even training young white boys to be cadets, young soldiers. They pretend they're training just for fun. The government keeps the war a secret. They don't want white people scared."

"If the whites were to get scared," Baba said, "they'd leave."

"Exactly," said Mr. Chinyanga. "But instead of a smooth transition, the government prefers a bloodbath."

Blessing glanced at Caleb. He sat with his mouth hanging open. Would this talk give him nightmares?

Mr. Chinyanga twirled his glass. "I've come here because I'm concerned about my brother, Reverend. Without his earnings, his family is hungry. Won't you use your influence?" he asked. "You're a respected pastor. Surely . . ."

Baba shook his head. "I'm sorry, but I don't know anyone in power."

"You keep to yourself, Reverend. Perhaps your approach is too cautious. If you are not going to befriend anyone in government, what about taking a risk, aligning yourself with ZAPU or ZANU?"

Blessing sucked in his breath. These were the Communist parties! The Communists wanted to start nuclear war. They wanted to blow up the whole world. Talk had it they were responsible for the Kingsley Fairbridge Road killing.

Baba shook his head again. "My path is the path of peace."

"Peace is too wishy-washy, Reverend. The *government* doesn't walk the path of peace." Mr. Chinyanga knocked lightly on the table, rocking it again.

"You and I both strive for liberation, brother. We walk the same path, though with different feet."

"But my brother's still in jail." Mr. Chinyanga slid back abruptly in his chair.

Caleb dropped the chicken bone he'd been gnawing.

Blessing thought of taking Caleb outside. But he just had to listen. He had to know how people got taken off and imprisoned.

"The Reverend King and Gandhi spent time in jail," Baba said in a low voice. "It can be a noble thing."

Blessing gripped the edge of the table with both hands. Did this mean that *Baba* might go to jail?

Mr. Chinyanga grunted. "What about when Jesus overturned the tables of the money changers in the temple? That was utilizing the power of violence. And what about when Jesus said, 'I come with a sword'?"

Blessing looked at Baba and then at Mr. Chinyanga, then back at Baba. How would Baba answer that? Usually he would say the devil made people act violently. But how could he say that about *Jesus*?

Baba folded his arms across his chest. "It is true that Jesus employed violence when no other means was available. I'm not saying that that may not someday be the case here. But I still have faith that the methods of the Reverend King and Gandhi can be effective in Rhodesia."

"We'll see, Reverend." Mr. Chinyanga buttoned his jacket. "We'll see."

"I will add your brother's name to our prayer circle."

Mr. Chinyanga grunted again but didn't say another word.

A Discovery

"I don't want you wandering off today, Evan," Mom had said that Saturday morning. "Not until we know more about this killing."

That meant no launching of the raft. But with cadets, Evan had more to think about than the raft. He'd relax at the print shop with Blessing.

In the storeroom behind the printing press, Blessing lifted the carton of ink rollers so that Evan could pull out the box of old postage stamps.

Evan carried the box to a table near the paper cutter and took off the lid. He fingered the stamps, canceled with round blue circles. "Look," he said, "a leopard."

"And this." Blessing held up a tiny portrait of the white explorer Kingsley Fairbridge.

"Let's put them in rainbow order first," said Evan.

When they'd laid out the stamps—red through purple, the grays and browns piled to the side—they shuffled them up again.

"By pictures this time," Blessing said.

They organized the stamps in rows of plants, animals, and people, including kings and queens.

"We've done this too many times," said Evan at last, stifling a yawn.

"Yeah, it's boring," Blessing agreed.

"Let's get scraps," Evan suggested, scooping the stamps back into the box. His hand caught on the rough wood, and he picked at a splinter.

The rubbish bin was filled with leftover bits from the paper cutter. These scraps were good for making cartoon books. But, best of all, the scraps could be clipped to the spokes of a bike to make it sound like a motorcycle.

"Luckily, Mr. Njopera did a lot of cutting," Evan said.

"Here's some green. Caleb likes green."

"Grab that bright yellow too. And the stiff stuff."

Suddenly, Evan spotted a sheet of peacock-blue paper under the paper cutter. He ducked down to get it, crawling through the dust on his hands and knees.

When he turned the sheet over, he stared at the black silhouette of an armed African soldier.

This was it.

The handbill.

The paper shook in his hands.

He, Evan M. Campbell, had found exactly what Colonel Rollins wanted.

He took a deep breath. How on earth?

"What did you find?" Blessing asked.

"Nothing." Evan folded the page in half and took another deep breath. If he showed the handbill to Blessing, he'd have some explaining to do.

Evan folded the handbill again.

Blessing began to pace in front of the paper cutter.

With each of Blessing's steps, Evan's breath tightened.

He folded it again. Good friends didn't keep secrets.

The handbill was almost small enough. It was just what he needed. Evan folded it one more time and tucked it into his pocket.

Blessing paused in his pacing.

Evan peeked out to see Blessing's brown feet, his dusty toes. He knew he should take the handbill out of his pocket, unfold it, and show it to Blessing. Tell him all about cadets. About the challenge to become a hero. But what then? Once he'd revealed his plan, he couldn't carry it out.

Evan put his hand over the folded handbill. Inside, he felt his heart thumping away. Warning him.

"Are you ever coming out from under there?" Blessing asked.

"Just a *sec*!" Evan called. "I'm trying to get a nasty splinter out of my finger!"

Clickety-Click

Outside the press building, Blessing knelt to unclip the soggy old paper from the spokes of his bicycle. He crumpled the used paper and put it in his bike basket. He tore the new stuff into pieces the right size, then attached them with clothespins, pinching his finger once. Even though mosquitoes bit his ankles, he worked on.

He set aside a pile of green for Caleb, noticing that Evan was riding in circles, the blue-gum seeds popping under his tires. Around and around he went, flicking the lever that rang his bell, ringing and ringing without stopping.

When the new cards were installed, Blessing hopped on his own bike. "Stop that noise," he said, "so I can hear." He took a trial spin. The spokes clacked slow or fast, depending on how he rode. Why didn't Evan care that he still had the old cards, which only made a soft slapping noise?

"Those cards are like the stamps," Evan said. "Boring. Let's go to the tuckshop and get a Coca-Cola."

"The tuckshop's closed. Let's ride down to the river."

"Naw." Evan kept circling, as though he couldn't stop, even on this lazy, steamy day.

"We could sort out our rock collections. I have a green one I want to trade."

"Naw," Evan repeated. He popped up his bike, lifting one wheel into the air.

Ever since Evan had come out from under the paper cutter, he'd been acting funny. Every now and then, he took one hand off the handlebars to pat something in his pocket.

"What *is* that?" Blessing asked. He got off his bike and took a step toward Evan.

"Nothing." Evan skidded to a stop and covered the pocket with his hand.

"Looks like something."

"It's not." Evan took off again.

"Let's see, then."

"I told you, it's *nothing*," Evan said, scowling, then rode away, standing up on the pedals to go faster.

Just as Evan disappeared around the corner, Blessing saw an unfamiliar Land Rover driving in the direction of the missionaries' houses. Who could it be?

Blessing kicked up the kickstand on his bike, got on, and followed.

The Land Rover stopped in front of the Bloomquist house. A man with short hair got out. He carried a briefcase and walked briskly.

Blessing waited while the man rang the doorbell, and Mr.

Bloomquist came to the door. The stranger displayed something inside the front of his jacket, and Mr. Bloomquist let him in.

Blessing lingered outside. Was Mr. Bloomquist about to be arrested? The stranger had that air about him. But that couldn't be. White people never got arrested. Probably the man was about to haul off an African and was stopping in first to take afternoon tea with the Bloomquists.

Cop in Doorway

Evan stared at a page of the novel *The Ship*. At first he'd been excited by the book's title, but the story opened with a boring scene of a sailor picking corned beef out of his teeth. And, besides, there was something far more important to think about.

Who had used the Mission press to print the peacock-blue handbill? How could he find out? And if he did learn who, what exactly would he do with the information?

"Look here," said Dad.

Evan glanced at one of Mr. Deaton's political cartoons. Above the cartoon was written an African saying: "When two elephants fight, it is the grass underneath that suffers." The cartoon itself was of a white man and an African each holding drawn guns. The "grass" was made up of tiny people, both African and white, their miniature faces streaked with tears.

"Is that about the liberation war, the *chimurenga*?" Evan asked.

Dad nodded. He tapped the cartoon. "A great political statement. Too bad the newspaper won't be able to print it."

Someone knocked at the front door. Who could it be so late in the evening? Dad turned over the cartoon, and Mom set down the crochet hook. She tucked away the afghan she'd been making for the orphan project.

Dad, in his undershirt and with his belt loosened, opened the door to a man wearing a suit and carrying a briefcase. The man's blond hair was cut so short that his pink scalp showed through.

"Criminal Investigation Department," he said, peeling back his jacket to flash a badge.

Mom adjusted the scarf over her curlers and pushed Evan's homework to one side of the dining-room table.

Evan stood up. *The CID!* The CID men were secret agents like James Bond. Just wait until he told Blessing that the CID had come to his house!

Evan felt like making a James Bond–style joke—something like, *CID: Cop in Doorway!*—but the man looked so serious that Evan sat back down.

"Alfred Seymour." The man held out his hand. His eyes were as gray and hard as the river stones in Evan's rock collection.

As Evan studied the pattern on Mr. Seymour's tie—white designs like fireworks going off on dark-blue silk—he had a thought that made his hands clammy. Did Mr. Seymour know that he'd found the peacock-blue handbill? Was he here to arrest him for not telling? Would he punch him in the stomach or pull out a tiny gun?

Dad shook Mr. Seymour's hand, then yanked his belt in a notch.

Mr. Seymour slapped his briefcase onto the dining-room table, ruffling Evan's homework papers. He sat down, took out a pen and notebook, narrowed his gray eyes, and said, "I'm here to investigate the killing on the Kingsley Fairbridge Road."

"We understand," Dad said. "How can we help?"

"By telling me all you know."

"We didn't know Mr. Stein," Mom said.

"You don't need to have known him to be of assistance, Mrs. Campbell," Mr. Seymour said.

Evan inched back in his chair. Mr. Seymour's gray eyes were like ice.

Mr. Seymour went on: "You may not be aware, Mr. and Mrs. Campbell, that your mission here has become a Communist hotbed."

Evan took a long, deep breath. *Communism.* Everyone was now talking about it. Communism was no longer in faraway Russia or China, but here in Rhodesia. Was it really right here, on the Mission?

A cuckoo bird came out of the clock, calling the hour.

When the cuckoo had slid back through the tiny doorway, Mom said, "You're wrong, Mr. Seymour. The Africans here aren't Communists. They're good Christians."

Mr. Seymour smiled and shook his head.

Dad added, "I'm afraid you're barking up the wrong tree, sir."

Mr. Seymour's close-cropped hair made him look like a dog with mange. Evan laughed nervously at the image, then choked the laugh back.

Mr. Seymour tapped the pen three times on the notebook. "This is no laughing matter, son. And"—he faced Dad—"I need to bark up *all* the trees."

Evan bit the inside of his cheek.

"You'd be surprised at how so-called Christianity and Communism go hand in hand," Mr. Seymour went on. "Many ministers who seem to be God-fearing support the cause of Communism." Mr. Seymour opened his briefcase. He reached inside. "I have something to show you."

He brought out the familiar peacock-blue paper that Evan couldn't stop thinking about. He handed it to Dad.

Evan's breath caught in his throat like a wad of cotton.

At the sight of the armed soldier, Mom gasped softly.

Dad held the handbill by the edges, as if it would contaminate him. "Surely this has nothing to do with the *Mission,*" he finally said.

"None of you knows anything about this?" Mr. Seymour stared at Mom, then Dad. His gray eyes bored into Evan.

Evan folded his arms tight across his chest. He felt as though he were on the raft, tilting this way and that. At any second, he could be flung into deep water. He shook his head. "No, sir."

Mr. Seymour shut his notebook. "Very well, then." He pushed back from the table. Before he stood up, he said, "You missionaries believe that you're supporting the cause of freedom. Be careful it isn't Communism that reaps the benefits."

After Dad had closed the door behind Mr. Seymour, Evan said, "Is that man right, Dad? Is it because of Communism that the Africans are rising up?"

Dad ran his fingers through his hair. "That's a good question, son. Unfortunately, the Communists seem to have jumped on the bandwagon of a worthy cause."

Pulling her crochet project out of the basket, Mom said, "The Communists may be the ones sabotaging our efforts toward a peaceful liberation."

"So the Communists *are* here?" Evan asked.

"It would seem so," Dad said.

"But on the *Mission*?" Evan persisted.

"That's a possibility."

In his room, Evan pulled his collection of rocks out from under the bed and opened the lid. The box contained fool's gold from a river, a piece of granite he'd found on a camping trip with Blessing in the Chimanimani Mountains, and an assortment of brown-and-gray lumps.

Underneath the rocks was the handbill, folded and pinched very small.

Evan took the packet out. He smoothed each folded edge between his thumb and forefinger.

He'd stumbled onto something as big and touchy as a nuclear bomb.

But, like Mr. Seymour, Evan didn't yet know everything. He was one step ahead of him and Colonel Rollins: he knew that the handbill had been printed here at the Mission. But by whom? That was what really mattered.

Once he knew, he'd catch that Communist. And after that, everyone at school, including Colonel Rollins and the boys who had once been his friends, would have to look up to him.

An Airplane

Blessing sat outside, listening to crickets and watching the headlights of the cars passing on the road. Overhead, the *mupuranga* trees whispered secrets.

One pair of headlights didn't pass on. Those came closer. And closer, until the lights shone into the yard, onto the front of the house. Blessing put up a hand, blinded.

He stood to look at that Land Rover, his eyes adjusting again to the gloom outside the headlights. On the side he saw the government symbol, a lion—holding a sword, ready to fight.

He ran inside. "Baba! Mai!" The police had never come to the house before. Blessing thought of Gladman's uncle and how he had once driven a delivery truck and now sat in jail.

He thought of how the police were scouring the countryside for the killers.

With Mai and Caleb and Mbuya, Blessing watched from the doorway as Baba went out to meet the officers.

They talked and Blessing tried to hear those muffled words.

Was this how it had happened with Gladman's *baba*? Baba wasn't screaming. Should he be? Blessing wondered if *he* should be screaming.

Baba waved and got into the backseat of the Land Rover.

He kept waving as the Land Rover drove away.

Blessing watched as the red taillights disappeared down the road, until there was nothing but blue-gum trees waving in the night.

Blessing walked this way, then that.

Caleb started crying. He clung to Mai's skirt.

Mai cried and clung to Mbuya.

Caleb needed help. Blessing gathered a cob from the maize, a few leaves, blades of elephant grass.

He took Caleb's hand and led him inside. "Come, *mununʼuna.* I'll make you an airplane."

Caleb sniffled and wiped his eyes with the back of his hand.

As Blessing made a fuselage from the cob, he told Caleb, "Baba will come back, Caleb. You'll see."

As he made the wings from leaves, he told Caleb, "Baba won't be gone long."

"But what about Gladman's *baba*?" Caleb asked.

"Our *baba* is an important man. They have to let him go. They have to," Blessing told him, twisting elephant grass into the shape of a propeller.

"Zoom, zoom!" Blessing flew the airplane over Caleb's head twice before he let him catch it.

"This airplane can go get Baba and bring him back," said Caleb, flying the plane through the room.

"Go, Caleb," said Blessing, forcing a smile. "Go get him now."

A Giant Eyeball

After Mr. Seymour left, Evan sat on the edge of his bed, wishing that he could play James Bond. He longed for the days when he and Blessing goofed around, inventing silly spy gadgets. But the sleuthing he was about to undertake was serious business, not a game. The stakes were very high.

A simple mask would have to do. Evan went to a drawer and got out a blue sweater. With scissors from his desk, he cut off one sleeve. In the sleeve, he slit holes for the eyes and one big hole for the nose and mouth.

Then he sat down on his bed again. What if the printer of the handbill was one of the killers? What if he got caught? James Bond always had a clever way out. But was he himself that clever? In a crunch, could he, Evan Campbell, slip out of a pair of handcuffs, fight his way out of a dungeon, escape a dozen pursuers?

◆ ◆ ◆

Late that night, when he was sure that Mom and Dad were asleep, Evan snuck out of bed, then tiptoed down the hallway and out of the house.

The moon was waxing in a clear sky, so he kept to the shadows. The air rang with the sounds of crickets and frogs.

At the base of the ancient fig tree, Evan pulled on the mask.

He climbed onto a low branch, the leaves shining in the moonlight like enormous hands. Poisonous green caterpillars lived on those leaves.

Perched in the crook of a branch, Evan peeled the hot mask up to eye level and kept shifting into the shadows, out of range of the moon, which was like a giant eyeball searching for him.

In his head, he recited the twenty-third Psalm: "*The Lord is my shepherd. . . .*" Finally, he just waited, drifting in and out of sleep.

He woke to a sound: footsteps on the dusty road. Soft and rhythmic. He peered into the night. A figure moved through the shadows. The figure paused, then approached the small building of the press. The doorknob clicked, and the figure stepped inside. The door closed with a gentle snap. But instead of pulling the chain for the light, the person turned on a flashlight and held it low.

Evan's blood raced.

He inched out of the tree, scraping his forearm in the slide down the trunk.

Once down, he crept like a leopard over the fig leaves, trying not to crunch.

He drew closer to the window.

He heard the grinding sound of the hand-fed press.

The person's flashlight still pointed downward. Would he never see the face?

The figure, and the way it moved, were familiar.

Suddenly the flashlight fell and shone upward.

It shone onto peacock-blue paper.

It shone into the crazy eyes of Gladman Chinyanga, the leader of the Bible students.

As the moonlight seeped through his mosquito net, Evan lay awake—his heart still pounding—mulling over the night's discovery.

He would never have guessed that Gladman, leader of the Bible-study group, was a Communist.

But it made sense—Gladman, the apprentice, who knew how to run the press.

Somehow Gladman was connected with the Communist terrorists lurking in the hills. He was using the Mission press to further their cause.

Was he acting alone? Or was his Shumba part of the plot, a link between the Mission and the freedom fighters?

As the moon slipped behind a tree, Evan wondered briefly if he should alert someone here on the Mission—Blessing's father, his own father, Mr. Njopera—instead of Colonel Rollins. But would they know how to keep the nation safe from Communism?

And would he get a medal? No. He'd get a pat on the back instead. Life at school would go on being miserable.

Again, Evan tasted that peppery flying ant.

Whispers

Blessing lay awake, listening for a sound that would signal Baba's return. Might it be the tires of the Land Rover rolling into the yard, the purr of the big engine? Or might it be Baba calling out, "I'm home!"?

Baba *would* come home, wouldn't he? Blessing thought of Mr. Chinyanga. . . .

Just as he'd begun to doze, Blessing heard the front door close softly. He got up, tucking the blanket around Caleb, and walked down the short hallway. The concrete floor was smooth under his bare feet.

In the living room, a low lamp was on, and Mai stood silhouetted near the doorway with Baba.

He'd come home! Thank the Lord! Baba was home again! But Blessing didn't dare step closer. This was obviously a private time for his parents.

Waiting in the shadows, he watched as they sat down on the sofa. Baba lowered his face into his hands.

Mai whispered, "Are you all right? What happened to you?"

"Just questioning. The Kingsley Fairbridge Road affair." His voice, traveling through the gaps between his fingers, was muffled.

"Did they hurt you?"

Blessing flinched at the question, but Baba shook his head.

Sitting side by side, the two didn't talk further. Outside, the crickets cried and a night bird called.

Blessing stayed in the dark hallway, reassuring himself that this was no dream. He wiggled his toes, feeling his feet solidly under him. His family was complete again, under one roof. Baba was home.

Then Baba raised his face, looked into the darkness, and said, "Come here, son."

Blessing crossed the small room. He eased himself onto the sofa next to Baba. "I'm glad you're back," he said.

"I am too, son. The Lord watched over me." With a loud sigh, Baba took Blessing's hand and Mai's hand, saying, "Let us pray."

Handkerchiefs

Evan arrived late at Cyril's birthday party, clutching his present.

That morning, Mrs. Cherryman had called Mom, inviting Evan.

"I don't want to go this year," Evan said. He was still reeling from last night's discovery.

"You must," Mom had insisted. "In a small community, it doesn't do to snub people."

Because it was Sunday and the British shops were closed, Mom had taken him to the Hindu part of town. Abudula & Sons had nothing a thirteen-year-old boy would like. Not only was Evan forced to go to the party, but he'd had to settle for taking a box of white handkerchiefs.

"Come in, dear," said Mrs. Cherryman. She wore a flowered frock and a small string of pearls. "The boys are already in the pool."

She led him through the living room, where a photograph of Queen Elizabeth hung next to a black-and-white photo of a young-looking Mr. Cherryman in military uniform.

The house stank of cigarette smoke.

Following Mrs. Cherryman, Evan thought of all the happy times he'd spent here in this house. If all could only be as it had been!

In the turquoise pool, Cyril and Graham rode on the shoulders of Adrian and Robert, trying to knock each other off. Johan dove under water. Purple bougainvillea spilled over the wall beyond. A Beatles song blared from the record player.

"Put on your swimming costume, Cowboy," called Cyril.

"Didn't bring one," Evan called back. He wished he'd remembered—the water looked refreshing. He put the present on the stack. Better to have brought nothing at all, but Mom had insisted.

Waiting for Cyril to offer him a swimming costume, he sat on the side, tapping his foot to the music.

"Wish some girls were here," said Johan.

"Know any?"

"My cousin Kate."

"Ring 'er up."

Evan took off his sandals and put his feet in the pool.

Graham, then Adrian, splashed him.

"More than one way to get wet," said Robert, laughing and blowing water from his mouth.

Evan shook spit from his hair, then moved to a chair. That did it. His mind was made up. This would be the last day of such treatment. Tomorrow he would show them all. Even if he had to hide his face on the Mission forever, he would unleash his secret.

After five more Beatles songs, an African maid brought out

green jelly molded like a star and a white cake. The frilly icing made the cake look like a girl's.

The maid set the food down on the round table under an umbrella decorated with balloons and streamers.

"Time to eat," sang out Mrs. Cherryman.

The boys climbed from the pool, dripping and bundling into towels.

Mrs. Cherryman lit the thirteen candles.

They sang loudly and off-key, drawing out the *"Dear Cyril . . ."*

"We hope you live to be a million . . ." sang Robert as Cyril blew out the candles.

"And then one million more . . ." finished Johan.

Cyril cut the cake, and Mrs. Cherryman added a scoop of lime jelly.

Evan pushed the sweet icing to the side. He spooned down the wobbly jelly.

It was time to open presents. The first was a hunting knife, from Adrian. When Cyril passed it around, Robert ran his index finger along the sharp edge, testing the blade. A thin red line appeared on his finger.

"Whoa, a knife. Oooh, blood," Evan said. He wished he could dive to the bottom of the pool and stay there. Why hadn't he thought to buy Cyril a present earlier? He could have gotten him an airplane that really flew, controlled by a battery-powered remote control.

After Cyril opened the Beatles 45s from Robert, he jumped up and put on a new tune.

Graham's present was a BB gun. Cyril aimed it at each of them—*bam-bam*—lingering, it seemed, on Evan.

By tomorrow, when Evan was a hero, Cyril would be happy to get even handkerchiefs from Evan Campbell. But now, while everyone was admiring the zebra-skin belt from Johan, Evan slipped the box of handkerchiefs under the chair cushion.

Boing, Boing

The air was fragrant with wood smoke as Blessing fed the chickens, scattering vegetable peelings over the dirt, which Mbuya had swept clean.

Hearing the sound of bike tires, he turned to see Evan ride up.

Evan dismounted and leaned his bike against a flamboyant tree. He dropped down on the vinyl car seat that served as a bench, saying, "I'm beat. I rode hard all the way here."

Blessing flung the last of the vegetable peelings to the chickens.

"The CID came to our house," Evan said, shifting his weight forward on the seat. "The guy had a badge." He gestured as though opening his coat, flashing a badge. "It was just like having James Bond in our dining room. Did the CID come to *your* house?"

"Baba was taken to police headquarters," Blessing said, his face suddenly stiff.

"Oh, no! Did he get arrested?"

"He's a pastor. They took him nicely." But it hadn't felt nice. Not at all.

"Was it because of the killing? Did they ask him who he thought was to blame?"

"I don't know." Blessing shrugged. Evan wanted all the gory details. He didn't care about Baba. Evan could be such an idiot sometimes.

"Your dad must sympathize with the killers," said Evan.

Blessing stared down at the dust underfoot, the random bits of gravel. "That's easy for you to say," he said. "You're white."

Evan sat back, his arms crossed. "Did they treat him badly?"

"They didn't *hurt* him."

Evan jabbed at a coiled spring that poked through the tan vinyl of the seat. "Hey, what's this?"

"It's a spring, can't you see?" Blessing said. Just because everything at Evan's house was in good repair, he needn't remark on what was broken elsewhere.

"Boing, boing." Evan poked at the spring.

"You'll just make it pop out more doing that," Blessing said. He tossed the rest of the vegetable peelings toward the chickens, who scattered, squawking. Then he threw the basket itself, raising a swirl of dust. "You're all just . . . just a bunch of white imperialists," he blurted out. "All of you. You're the same as the others."

"Not me." Evan stood up. "I'm not like that."

"You're not?" Blessing walked off, kicking the blue-gum seeds, his heart flaming.

007

On Monday morning, Colonel Rollins was sitting at his desk in the classroom, the students' pile of Rhodesian maps before him. He glanced up, then back down. "What is it, Campbell?"

"I have something to report, sir." Evan lifted his hand in salute. "Something urgent."

"Well, then"—Colonel Rollins eyed him—"close the door."

Evan shut it hard, as though the firm sound would silence the stream of protest in his head: *What would Martin Luther King say about turning in Gladman? What would Blessing say?*

Just yesterday Blessing had called him a white imperialist. Now, it seemed, Blessing was right.

Colonel Rollins leaned his elbows on the pile of maps. "What's on your mind, lad?"

Evan paused, swallowed hard, then rushed on: "I found something at the Mission printing press." He unfolded the peacock-blue handbill.

Colonel Rollins whistled. He took the handbill from Evan, saying, "At the press, eh? Did someone on the Mission print it, then?"

"There's a group called the Shumba. It's supposed to be a Bible-study group. The leader is the one who printed the handbill, sir."

"You know this for a fact?"

"Yes, sir." Evan said the words firmly, quelling the trembling in his stomach.

"Very well, then. Let's go down to Headmaster Cork's office."

Proceeding down the hallway, Evan steadied himself. He listened to the ring of his footsteps, each solid and loud. He was a kid James Bond. He, the Yank missionary, had found and was sharing information—like an enemy's secret code—that no other cadet had.

He *was* doing the right thing.

Colonel Rollins carried the blue handbill like a banner.

The door to Headmaster Cork's office stood open, revealing walls lined with books. A photograph of the queen, her crown glittering with jewels, hung to the right of the window.

Mr. Cork sat behind his massive desk of *mukwa* wood as though behind a barricade. "Come in, gentlemen," he said as Evan and Colonel Rollins paused in the doorway.

Evan hesitated, his belly trembling again. Yet it was too late to retreat.

With a flourish, Colonel Rollins laid the handbill on the headmaster's desk, saying, "Campbell found this at his mission, sir. An African printed it."

Mr. Cork picked up the handbill, his glasses slipping to the end of his nose. "My God," he said. "It's the one we've already seen, isn't it. This was found on the *Mission*?"

Outside, the brass bell rang for uniform inspection. Mr. Cork made no move to get up. Instead he uncapped a fountain pen and, stroking his giant mustache, made notes.

Evan wished he could read what Mr. Cork was writing.

At last, Mr. Cork paper-clipped his notes to the handbill, saying, "This is exactly the information we need. You have been of great service to the nation, lad."

Evan stood taller.

Later that morning, Headmaster Cork came into the classroom. "No need to stand, lads." He gestured for everyone to sit. "I need to take Campbell for a spell. Leave your things here, Campbell."

Evan straightened his tie. Was he about to be honored? If so, why alone?

Two police officers—one blond, the other with sandy-brown hair—stood in the hallway, dressed in khaki uniforms.

Evan suddenly grew light-headed. He pinched his nails into his palms.

The blond officer stepped forward. "I'm Officer Cowles. You'll need to come to headquarters."

"For a bit of questioning," added the sandy-haired man. "My name's Officer Roebuck."

Evan took a step back. He hadn't counted on having to deal with actual *police.*

The khaki-colored police Land Rover had a lion holding a sword emblazoned on the side. Riding through Umtali, Evan shielded his face with his hat, as though from the sun. No one from the Mission must see him!

"Meyers shot three dassies last weekend," said Officer Cowles.

Officer Roebuck laughed. "Lot of good that'll do him. Can't mount a dassie head on the wall. He ought to bag himself a kudu."

Headquarters was a neat white building with a tidy, trimmed yard. Two constables with tall bucket-shaped hats stood on guard.

Inside, a receptionist sat behind a desk with a portrait of the queen in a stand-up frame.

"This way, lad," said Officer Cowles.

Evan was led to a room with leather swivel chairs. Through the bars on the windows, he saw trees outside. He heard someone clipping the bushes. Might he soon be locked away in a room with bars like these?

Sometimes Dad stopped on the way to Salisbury so that Evan could play on the swinging footbridge that crossed a gorge. Evan liked to jump up and down, making the bridge sway and undulate. Sometimes his own jump rippled back to him unexpectedly, making the bridge swing so wildly that he had to hold on tightly to the cable railings. Now, as Officer Roebuck pulled out a pad of paper, Evan remembered the bridge. He could almost feel its unpredictable motion. His hands grew clammy, his throat tight.

It occurred to him that Gladman wouldn't be invited to step down the hall with a "This way, lad." He'd be handcuffed and shoved rudely along.

"So, what do you have for us, lad?"

Evan wished he could lean back in the chair, relaxed and confident, the way Agent 007 reported to his superiors. If he could pretend to be James Bond, he wouldn't have to think of how he was acting even worse than his classmates. He wasn't just *talking* ill of Africans; he was *doing* ill. "The handbill, sir, the one I turned in—I found it under the paper cutter. Late the other night, I spied on the printing press and saw an African printing more copies." He wiped his damp hands on his shorts.

Officer Roebuck looked up. "Spell the man's name, please, lad." His pen hovered over a blank sheet of paper.

"G-L-A-D-M-A-N is his first name. His surname is C-H-I-N-Y-A-N-G-A."

As Evan spelled the name, it was as though he were closing an envelope tight, plunging a seal into hot wax. With each letter, he sealed Gladman's fate.

The officer wrote the name in block letters.

Evan read the words upside down. "He's a Communist, sir," he added.

"Obviously," said Officer Roebuck.

"You are a very brave young man," said Officer Cowles.

"Very mature," said Roebuck, putting down the pen.

"Just doing my duty as a citizen, sirs." Evan plunged his sweating hands deep into his pockets.

Okra

Blessing tied the bag of okra onto the back of his bike. The okra was fresh from his family's farm. He lifted Caleb onto the handlebars and pedaled off. The spokes clicked with card stock.

"Hang on tight!" Blessing said in Caleb's big ear. "We're going around a curve."

"Whee!" Caleb said as his knuckles went white.

The first stop was the Deatons'. Their house helper, Violet, bought five handfuls of okra. Blessing stuffed the coins deep in his pocket.

The Bloomquists didn't answer their door—front or back.

Blessing pedaled on to try the Richardsons, who said they didn't care for okra, and to Mr. Ford, who brought a bowl to the door and filled it up.

When Blessing got to the Campbells' house, he gave Grace some okra. When she tried to pay, Blessing said, "Oh, no, Grace. This okra is a present for the Campbells."

"Why, thank you, Blessing. How's the ride, Caleb?"

Caleb giggled.

"Is Evan home?" Blessing balanced on the bicycle, scuffing at the dirt with his toes.

"He is. But he says he's not to be disturbed."

"Not even by *me*?"

"Not even by you."

Was it because of the fight they'd had the other day? Was Evan holding a grudge? Blessing felt ashamed of the way the flame had risen in his heart. He'd burned the air with his words, burned his best friend. "Is Evan sick?"

"He doesn't seem to be." Grace put a hand on his shoulder. "Don't worry, Blessing. He'll come around soon."

"Tell him I was here, then."

Blessing put his foot on the pedal and pushed off. He'd wanted to share a story about Burly Ford. Mr. Ford always put his shoes onto the *stoep* to be shined. But last night someone, instead of shining them, had smeared them with cow dung. He himself had had mean thoughts about Mr. Ford, but now someone had actually *done* something mean.

What could Evan be doing that was more important than hearing such a story?

By the time they reached the Gainsbys', there were only a few okra pods left.

Mrs. Gainsby herself came to the back door. "Oh, how cute you look today!" she cried, pinching Caleb's fat cheek. "You're a brave boy to ride like this." She helped herself to the last of the okra and handed Blessing some coins.

Now that the okra was gone, Caleb moved to the back of the bike.

Usually, Blessing liked to go wild on the way home, zipping and zooming, making Caleb laugh. But today he rode home slowly. Was Evan still so angry about their fight that he'd refused to see him?

The Launch

"It's Blessing," Mom called out from the front door that Saturday morning.

Evan walked down the polished wooden floor of the hallway, to see Mom in her flowered housecoat and, behind her, Blessing crossing the threshold.

Evan's walk slowed. The other day, with her hands on her hips, Grace said that Blessing had come with the okra. "Why didn't you want to go see him?" she'd demanded. "That's not how you treat a friend."

"I didn't feel well," Evan had replied.

Now he lifted a hand to Blessing. "Howzit," he said.

"Howzit," Blessing answered.

They stood together, Evan in the warm dimness of the house, Blessing halfway in and halfway out in the bright morning. Today he was not to be avoided.

Blessing rocked from one foot to the other; he looked down into his hands and then back up. "I'm sorry for calling you a white imperialist."

"That's okay. Sorry about your dad. I'm glad he's back."

"He's finally like his old self," said Blessing. He rocked back and forth again. "Can we launch the raft today?"

Evan hesitated. If only he could put off the launch. In the past few days, his life had gotten so complicated. Launching a bunch of bamboo lashed to old tires felt too simple.

Yet he'd made a promise to Blessing.

"Sure," Evan said. "Come in and eat breakfast first, though."

Dad was already seated for breakfast, his tie flipped over his shoulder to keep it out of his porridge. "Sit down, boys," he said.

Grace hurried to set another place.

"Now that we're all here, let's pray," said Dad.

They joined hands, Mom pulling Grace into the circle.

"Heavenly Father," Dad began, "bless this food and the hands that prepared it. . . ."

The air smelled of hot tea mixed with the scent of pink table roses: spicy and sweet. "Amen," Evan responded.

Dad moved the plate of sliced mangoes closer to Blessing. "Put a little weight on your bones, *mwanangu.*"

Grace poured tea, the spout of the teapot clinking against the china cups.

Blessing dumped several spoonfuls of sugar into his tea and several more onto his porridge.

Evan lingered over his own porridge, half wishing that they'd never found that raft in the high grass up by the pond.

◆ ◆ ◆

In the backyard, Evan wheeled the wheelbarrow out from the toolshed. Together, he and Blessing hoisted up the bulky raft. With a loud creak, it shifted, and a bamboo pole came loose.

"Leave it," said Evan as Blessing bent over. "One less won't matter."

"Too bad we can't tie the raft onto the wheelbarrow," said Blessing.

Evan ran through the possibilities in his head. Rope? More inner tubes? But all that sounded like too much trouble. "We'll just have to be careful," he said.

Going uphill, the raft felt much heavier than it had going down. Each bump threatened to shake it off. After it had crashed into the bushes three times, Evan said, "Let's just leave it here."

"Leave it?" Blessing asked. "Why would we do that?"

So Evan squatted down beside Blessing, once again dragging up the flimsy contraption of bamboo and tires.

They worked together, shoulder to shoulder, while the sun burned a hole in the sky.

Halfway, they stopped again at the loquat tree. As Evan slowly chewed the yellow fruit, he wished that he was doing anything but this. He wished that he was alone in his room with a stack of comics. *The Beezer, Jag,* and *Cyclone* were all filled with exotic excitement that had nothing to do with Evan's real life.

Suddenly, Blessing pointed at Evan's chest, asking, "What's that?"

Evan looked down at the bulge under his shirt. He'd been unprepared for Blessing's unexpected visit and was still wearing the cadet compass. He pulled out the silver disk, saying, "It's just a compass."

Blessing's eyes grew wide. "Can I hold it?"

Evan lifted the strap over his head.

Blessing clicked the silver case open and shut, open and shut.

The right thing to do, Evan thought—something that would relieve his guilt—would be to give Blessing the compass. But it was part of his cadet uniform. "Thou shalt not covet," he joked.

"I shan't," Blessing responded, slowly laying the compass on Evan's open hand.

When they finally arrived at the pond, they guided the wheelbarrow over the narrow dam.

"If the raft falls off here, we're sunk," said Evan.

"Sunk, thunk, plunk," said Blessing.

"Shhh. I can't concentrate."

When they finally arrived at the other side, Evan dropped his handle. "Stop."

"Blackjack seeds in your socks again?"

"No. I mean, yes. But that's not why we have to stop. We have to tie these on our feet." He pulled four plastic bags from his pocket.

"Because of bilharzia?"

"Exactly."

No one wanted to get the parasite, which lived in African waters.

They took off their shoes and fastened the plastic bags around their ankles with rubber bands that Evan had brought. There was an advertisement for boys' underpants on the bags.

Evan lifted a small, round bottle of Pond's cold cream from the grass.

Blessing laughed. "Who's been washing her face up here?"

"Look what kind it is," said Evan, putting his finger on the word *Pond's*. "Where else would anyone use it?" He tried to open the bottle, but the lid was jammed. But now he had an idea. "When they launched the *Queen Elizabeth*, they broke a bottle of champagne over the bow."

"But face cream is nothing like champagne," Blessing objected.

"But we have to christen our raft." Evan smacked the thick glass bottle against the bamboo. The bamboo rattled, yet the bottle didn't break.

He cracked the bottle open against a rock. He reached in around the jagged glass and scooped some of the gooey white cream. He spread it over the old tires, saying, "Now they'll have nice complexions."

"You mean white ones," Blessing said.

"Ha!"

Evan waded into the pond first, pulling the raft behind him, the underwater grass tangling around his ankles.

When the raft was floating, Evan counted, "One . . . two . . . three . . . go!" and they jumped on.

"Row, row, row your boat," Evan sang.

"We can't row without oars," Blessing said.

Evan pretended to row anyway, moving his arms up and down.

With a glugging sound, the raft sank a little. Bubbles rose from the ends of the bamboo poles.

"We're shipwrecked!" Blessing said.

"Row, row . . ." Evan still sang, but slower. How could the raft be going down so soon?

After a final glug, they were waist deep in mud.

"Bilharzia!" Blessing shouted, scrambling to land.

Evan scrambled up too, his eyebrows drawn together. He scooped up a handful of dirt and threw it. "Stinking raft!" He threw another handful. "Stupid, stinking raft!"

They ripped the plastic bags off their feet and sat in the sun to dry, covered in red mud, eating the meat-loaf sandwiches that Grace had packed.

Evan swallowed a big bite, then took another. Of course the raft had sunk. It symbolized his friendship with Blessing. And now that he'd kept secrets, that friendship too was sinking.

"The stinking thing's sunk too deep to get out," said Evan.

"Yup," agreed Blessing. "I'm not getting back in there."

Evan threw his bread crusts into the pond. Fish came to the surface. "Stinker," he said, and pulled blackjacks from his wet socks.

Bullies

"Listen!" Blessing said.

Evan's hand—picking out blackjacks—froze.

A radio was playing *chimanje manje* music.

There, on the dam, blocking the way down, stood Kingsize, Lovemore, and Petrol. Slingshots stuck out of their back pockets. Petrol carried a transistor radio.

Blessing stood up and waved.

The boys ignored him, so Blessing tossed a rock into the pond.

He turned to see Evan crouched down behind the empty wheelbarrow. Was he playing a game? Blessing watched as Evan looked into the bush. Looked at the pond. Looked at the boys. Back at the bush.

"What's wrong?" Blessing asked.

"Shhh."

"Think they might make you eat another ant?" Blessing whispered.

"Shhh, I said."

Evan put on his shoes, then stood up and took hold of the wheelbarrow. Suddenly, he wheeled it onto the dam, pushing it like a battering ram.

Blessing followed.

"Hey, it's Pastor's Son and Bhunu taking a walk together," said Lovemore.

Petrol turned off the radio.

"*Iwe, mufana!* Hey, youngster," Kingsize said, stepping forward. His T-shirt sleeves were rolled up, a pack of cigarettes tucked into the fold. "Hey, what's this?" Kingsize lifted a hand to his face, touching his nose.

"Nose," Evan answered.

Why were his lips quivering? Was being teased that bad?

"And this?" asked Petrol, moving closer, pulling up his own shirt, and pointing.

Lovemore and Kingsize giggled.

"Belly button."

"How about this? What's inside here?" Lovemore reached down to his trousers and put a hand on his zipper.

"He's too white to have one," said Petrol.

"He doesn't even know what it is," Lovemore said.

Blessing kicked some dirt into the water. The boys were going too far.

With a jerk, Evan pushed the wheelbarrow forward, almost touching Petrol's knees, saying, "Let us pass."

"'Let us pass,'" said Lovemore in a high, girly voice.

Yet the three moved aside.

Right after they went by, Kingsize called out: *"Iwe, mufana, ndokurowa!"*

"I'll beat you up!" echoed Lovemore in English, then howled.

Evan almost ran down the path, the wheelbarrow clattering in front of him.

"Wait up!" Blessing called.

As Blessing walked home in the twilight, he passed Burly Ford's house. The lamp was on in the dining room, and Blessing saw Mr. Ford eating dinner, his house helper carrying a tray away from the table.

Blessing wondered again who'd smeared cow dung on Mr. Ford's shoes. Had it been a good-natured joke or something worse?

He felt bad about his own unkind feelings toward Mr. Ford. Yet, seeing him gesturing toward the house helper, he sensed his feelings surging even stronger within him.

He walked on quickly and thought instead of the boys up by the pond. They'd been threatening Evan, but not enough to make him such a nervous wreck. What if they *had* once made him eat a flying ant? Was that so terrible?

Yet Evan's hands had been shaking when he'd let Blessing take the handles of the wheelbarrow. Maybe he was just upset about the raft.

Remembering the way the raft had sunk, Blessing picked up a stick and hurled it so hard his armpit hurt.

In the distance behind him, Blessing heard the loud calls of the three big Shumba boys.

Ice-Cream Headache

Mom, dressed neatly in a lacy blouse, passed a pitcher of grape juice around the table. Blessing and his father had come to dinner.

Evan smelled meat cooking. He heard Grace bustling in the kitchen—opening the oven door, sliding the pan out.

Blessing filled his glass and handed the heavy pitcher on. He took a gulp, then stuck out his purple tongue, showing it off to Evan.

They laughed until the Reverend Mudavanhu frowned at Blessing.

With the white cloth napkin, Blessing wiped grape juice from his mouth.

The reverend addressed Mom and Dad: "Mai and Caleb will be envious when they hear about your fine cooking. They send their apologies, but my sister-in-law arrived from Mrewa unexpectedly."

Evan made a fist, and Blessing joined him in playing Rock-Paper-Scissors, both moving their hands stealthily so that the adults wouldn't notice.

"The training of the teachers is proceeding well," said Dad. "They are a bright, quick lot and should be able to take over soon."

"Good to hear," said the reverend, "but I'm not surprised."

"Yes, the missionary's job —" began Dad.

"— is to work himself out of a job," finished the reverend, chuckling.

Evan made a face at Blessing. The two dads were always saying things like that!

"We look forward to the day when Africans can run the Mission themselves," said Mom. "But, on another note, Reverend—how are *you*? You've had all of us anxious."

Blessing's hand—two fingers forming scissors to cut Evan's flat paper hand—froze in midair, then dropped to his lap.

The reverend moved his fork an inch to the left; his spoon, then his knife, an inch to the right. "The police are just doing their jobs, looking for the killers," he finally said.

"Still," said Dad, "it would have been more civilized of them to question you in your home."

"As the CID did us," Mom added.

Evan wished that the conversation hadn't turned this way. He was glad to see Grace bring a platter through the swinging doors from the kitchen. His mouth watered at the sight of the juicy meat.

Grace set down the platter, stuck the carving knife and big fork into the roast, put her hands on her hips, and said, "Gladman

Chinyanga has been arrested. My brother just came with the news."

Evan's forearms prickled as though poked with dozens of icy pins. The prickly feeling threatened to spread to his chest. He took a deep breath, willing the feeling to go away.

"What happened, Grace?" Dad asked, laying both hands flat on the table.

"The police drove up," Grace said, her hands now in her apron pockets. "Right by the bus stop. They took Gladman away in handcuffs."

Evan shuddered.

"You okay?" Blessing asked.

"Why wouldn't I be?" Evan swallowed hard. He focused on the carved elephant head next to a picture of Jesus kneeling to wash his disciple's feet.

He'd been fighting Communism. He had. He'd acted for the sake of the nation. For the sake of the Mission. For the good of his own family. Of Blessing's family.

The reverend looked around, saying, "I'd hoped it wouldn't come to the arrest and detention of one from our mission. Every Sunday I warn my congregation. . . ."

"Gladman is a relative of yours, isn't he?" Mom asked, looking first at the reverend, then at Blessing.

The reverend nodded.

"He is, Mai." Blessing answered.

"A distant cousin," the reverend added.

Very distant, thought Evan. Hardly a relative at all. A Communist. A Red. A genuine terrorist.

"The situation is dire," the reverend said. "Gladman's father has been in jail for months. The family is struggling without a breadwinner. And now Gladman too . . ."

Evan swallowed hard.

Grace went to the kitchen and returned with a bowl of boiled cabbage and a tomato salad.

The food sat in the middle of the table. No one touched it.

"Please eat," said Mom, handing the tomatoes to the reverend.

Dad carved the meat. He lifted thick slabs between the big knife and fork, transferring them onto the plates.

The loaded plates were handed down the table.

Evan pushed his food back and forth, his head swirling.

Finally, Grace took the plate away.

She brought ice cream with pink guava sauce, setting the dishes down with small clatters, breaking the silence.

Evan took one bite of the ice cream—just one—and got a headache like a searing spike in his forehead.

"I Have a Dream"

In science class, Blessing was winding copper wires around magnets to electrify his guitar. The guitar lay on the shelf, deliciously finished, just waiting.

He'd been looking forward to this day. Soon, with his electric guitar, he'd sound just like the Beatles. Yet he was having trouble focusing on the work. He kept pausing, gazing out at the bishop birds swooping through the blue sky, thinking of how Gladman had been arrested. Even though Gladman was the leader of the Mission Bible-study group, the police had taken him.

And they'd taken Baba for no reason. And returned him for no reason.

Blessing twisted the soft copper wire, securing it.

Who would be next?

Blessing sat between Gravy and Bright on the hard wooden bench. Beit Hall was filled with whistles, catcalls, and the knocking sound of benches being rocked back and forth — all magnified by echoes bouncing off the concrete walls.

Baba had surprised the whole school with a special treat: this afternoon they would view a newsreel of Dr. Martin Luther King giving his famous "I Have a Dream" speech. A big white screen had been lowered over the velvet curtains of the stage.

Blessing glanced back, to see Mr. Deaton and Mr. Campbell working with the projector. They leaned in close, adjusting the big metal reel.

"I hope they can concentrate, with all the noise," Blessing said to Gravy.

When someone turned the lights off, the catcalls and shrieks, the rock of the benches, grew so loud that Blessing covered his ears.

But as the image appeared on the screen, all grew magically silent. Blessing could feel his heart thud against his ribs. On either side of him, he heard the breathing of Bright and Gravy.

The newsreel opened with pictures of many people walking together, carrying signs and singing, *"We shall overcome."* Blessing stared at the white people among the Africans — *Negroes,* he corrected himself. There were almost as many whites coming to see the Reverend King as Negroes.

The Reverend King's huge face — many times bigger than life — appeared on the screen. He looked like an African, but he talked like the Campbells, like a Yank. Behind him was a gigantic stone statue of President Lincoln, the freer of the American slaves. The hairs stood up on Blessing's arms.

The camera showed shots of a long rectangular pool with thousands of people gathered on either side. In Rhodesia, an

African would never attract such a large crowd, especially of white people.

Although the Reverend King spoke of the American Negroes, when he said things like "An exile in his own land," it seemed to Blessing that he was speaking right to him.

Blessing stored up quotes like shining jewels.

At the end, when the Reverend King said, "Let freedom ring!" Blessing felt like lifting his own arm.

He savored all of it and memorized what he could.

Later, he would tell Evan everything. Not even Evan had seen "I Have a Dream."

The Star

Beyond the brown canvas tents, the Land Rovers were parked in a circle, firelight reflecting off the fenders. The promised camping trip was under way.

It was a clear night, and overhead, the Milky Way glowed, a broad band of soft radiance.

The air smelled of the pine logs burning in the fire ring.

Evan sat on a stump by the fire, dressed, like the others, in his cadet uniform. He'd laid out his bedroll in a tent, but no one else — not even the boys who barely knew him — had moved in.

So far, he was camping alone, in spite of his act of heroism. Wouldn't Colonel Rollins and Headmaster Cork ever tell the others he'd captured a Communist? Days had passed. Gladman had even been arrested.

Evan put a hand on his bare pocket. He'd been promised a medal.

"Do you think they're in the bush over there?" asked Graham, peering into the darkness.

"Terrs are everywhere," said Johan. "Commies wear red, so we'll spot them."

Other boys were running in and out of the bush, which pressed close on all sides.

"I saw a shooting star!" shouted Adrian.

"Look! There's another!"

"I just heard an elephant."

"More likely a lion," said Robert.

"Or a warthog farting, ha, ha!"

"Or Cherryman farting," muttered Evan.

"Gather round the fire, campers," said Colonel Rollins. "I have a special announcement." He threw more wood on, and sparks danced up.

Everyone gathered, including the chaperoning fathers and a group of swooping bats.

Dad had refused to be part of this outing, saying that he couldn't support cadets. Saying that even a campout wouldn't be innocent, given the military nature.

"We're not going to *kill* anyone," Evan had said.

"True, but they'll be wooing you with marshmallows."

At that point, Evan had remembered Gladman. Colonel Rollins might honor his brave deed at the campout. And Evan certainly didn't want Dad to hear about *that.*

"It's okay, Dad. There's enough fathers already," he'd said.

Cyril sat across the fire pit, throwing twigs into the blaze.

"Right here, Campbell," Colonel Rollins said, patting the log next to him.

As Evan scooted over, he straightened his knee-high socks. Was this to be the big moment?

Colonel Rollins sat silently while everyone settled. He poked at the fire with a long stick.

Maybe he wasn't going to make an announcement, after all.

But at last Colonel Rollins stopped stirring the coals. He looked around at the faces, ruddy in the firelight.

"The other day I spoke of terrorists," Colonel Rollins began. "I spoke of heroism, of looking for ways to protect our nation." He laid a hand on Evan's shoulder. "You will all be relieved to know that, thanks to our American friend, we've put a Communist away."

They all faced Evan, staring as though seeing him for the first time. Cyril's mouth hung open. Robert's eyebrows knitted together.

Evan stretched his legs toward the fire. A delicious warmth like thick, sweet honey flowed through him.

In the silence, a log fell into the flames, releasing a shower of dancing sparks.

"So who was it, Campbell?" Graham asked at last.

"A terrorist right on our mission," Evan answered.

"An African?" Adrian asked.

Evan nodded.

"All terrs are Africans," someone commented.

"Not true," said Evan. "The terrs are from Russia and China. Colonel Rollins said so."

Colonel Rollins held up a hand. When the boys quieted, he said, "Therefore, our first cadet to receive a medal is Evan Campbell."

Colonel Rollins took a box from his pocket.

As Evan watched, all seemed to proceed in slow motion: Colonel Rollins lifted the lid of the box. He tilted the box toward the firelight. He revealed a small bronze star.

Everyone drew close.

"Don't catch yourselves on fire, lads," said Johan's father.

Breathing heavily, Colonel Rollins pinned the bronze star on Evan's pocket.

"Congratulations, lad," said Mr. Cherryman.

"Fine work," Graham's father said.

The firelight made the medal twinkle.

Evan touched each sharp point. He felt the star's solid weight. Evidence of his heroism—the bit he'd done to stop Communism in its tracks—was right here, securely pinned over his beating heart.

Yet doubt flickered like firelight. *Had* justice been served?

James Bond never ended a spy adventure with these kinds of worries. He kissed a beautiful girl, and that was that.

As the boys ate bully beef and roasted mealies cooked on the *braivleis*, Evan guessed that each was pondering a way to get his own star.

After dinner, everyone sang "Kookaburra Sits in the Old Gum Tree" while Evan sat silently.

Overhead, the stars glittered like tiny cadet medals, twinkling, mocking.

Adrian and Robert, plus three boys Evan barely knew, had moved their bedrolls into his tent. Evan wished that Cyril had joined him in his moment of glory.

"Let us see that star," said one.

"Unpin it and pass it around," said another.

"I thought you were a kaffir lover," whispered Adrian.

"That was a dirty trick to play on an African from your mission," said Robert. "You must feel a bit funny about that."

Evan turned over in his sleeping bag. Robert was right.

In the bush, the jackals howled.

A Pastoral Visit

"Come with us," Blessing called out the window of the Land Rover. "We're going to the countryside today. We'll see places like my grandparents' farm."

"Lemme ask." Evan disappeared inside his house.

Blessing drummed his fingers on the armrest until Evan came out.

He climbed into the Land Rover, saying, "Good morning, Reverend," to Baba, who sat in the front seat, and, "Good morning, sir," to Mr. Chinyanga.

As Gladman's uncle drove out of the Mission gates and in the direction away from town, Blessing briefly wondered if Evan knew who Mr. Chinyanga was. Probably not. But it didn't matter—Mr. Chinyanga had no connection with Evan.

"Guess what," said Blessing. "Our whole school saw the 'I Have a Dream' speech."

"Dad told me. Was it good?

"It was great." Blessing could still see the Reverend King's big, comforting face rising on the screen before him. "There were Negro and white people marching together, sitting together. The white people seemed to want justice as much as the Negroes did. White policemen were protecting the Reverend King."

"Did it last long?"

"Not long enough. They had to play it three times before we had enough." Blessing went on to recount the details of the crowd that had gathered in front of the giant statue of Abraham Lincoln, with the Reverend King in front—the singing, the cheering and clapping, the air of excitement and hope. Whenever Evan asked a question, Blessing smiled and happily answered, until he had told everything.

When they turned off the main road onto a rutty dirt one, Mr. Chinyanga said, "Only a few more miles."

Blessing leaned his face out the window of the Land Rover. His whole body was filled with the memory of the Reverend King and with the green smell of mango trees, tall grass, and big, leafy bushes.

They passed kraals full of cattle, then fields of maize.

"Look at that," said Blessing, pointing to boys sitting in towers, watching for baboons. The towers were made of gum poles lashed together with *msasa*-tree bark.

Evan leaned over Blessing, sticking his head out too.

"If a troop of baboons comes to eat the crop, those boys'll shoot rocks from their slingshots," said Blessing.

Evan drew back an imaginary slingshot. "Kerpow!"

The car bounced across a stream, where naked children

splashed in the water, then entered the village. A little store called Shiri Yekutanga had a Lucky Strike cigarette sign out front. Teenagers sat on the *stoep,* smoking. A radio played loud *chimanje manje* music.

As Mr. Chinyanga drove between hedges of spiny euphorbia, he honked at a boy pushing a hoop with a stick. The hoop spun away, and the boy frowned.

"Poor boy," said Blessing. "I wouldn't like it if a car honked at *me*!" He waved at the boy. *If the Reverend King were here, he'd make things right for that boy.*

Evan waved too.

A big group of children chased the car, laughing and shouting.

Mr. Chinyanga stopped the Land Rover in front of a tiny round house made of mud and wattle. The house had no windows, and smoke came out the roof.

"Mrs. Chinyanga has to be very sad, with her husband and son both in jail," Blessing said.

"Who?" Evan asked.

"Gladman's mother."

Evan paused with his hand on the door handle. "Is that why we're stopping? I thought we were just going for a ride."

"Didn't know you cared."

"Well, I do," Evan said.

The slamming of car doors had brought a skinny tan dog to the gate, barking his head off. The cocks ran crowing in circles.

A woman slapped at the dog and cocks with a rag until the dog slunk away and the cocks hid under a dish-drying rack made of twigs. "Be still," she ordered.

Two little boys and a girl stood in the doorway, peeking out. Blessing waved at them. *Don't be afraid,* he felt like calling. Perhaps they thought the Land Rover had come to take someone away.

Walking to the gate, Mrs. Chinyanga said to Baba, *"Makadini, mufundisi."* She curtsied and clapped her hands in greeting.

Baba answered, *"Ndakasimba kana makasimbawo, mai,"* and Blessing, Baba, and Mr. Chinyanga answered with their own claps.

During the traditional Shona greeting, Evan stood with his hands in his pockets.

Mrs. Chinyanga opened the gate. "Come in, please. Come in."

Blessing stepped into the yard, which was dirt, swept clean of rocks. He looked around at a wrecked car, half covered with a tarp. There was a basket of dried mealie cobs, waiting to be ground, and a burlap bag full of peanuts.

He breathed in the smells of the countryside, saying to Evan, "Just like at my grandparents'."

Mrs. Chinyanga fumbled with a handkerchief, untying it. She picked out some coins. Giving the money to one of the boys, she told him: "Christopher, run buy a package of biscuits and a tin of milk."

Blessing whispered to Evan, "Mrs. Chinyanga has almost nothing in that handkerchief, yet she's buying things for our tea."

"We shouldn't . . ." began Evan.

Mrs. Chinyanga called to the other boy: "Albert! Bring the reverend a chair."

To the girl, she said, "Elizabeth! Put the teakettle on the fire."

Albert brought Baba a wooden chair. Blessing squatted with

the others, while Evan tried to coax the dog out from under the bush.

"We are here to offer our support, Mrs. Chinyanga," Baba said from the chair. "We've come to see how you are doing."

Mrs. Chinyanga sighed. "With my husband gone, life has been hard. The crops need tending." She sighed again. "The school fees are due."

Blessing watched as Evan turned from the dog and crossed the yard, to stand gazing at Mrs. Chinyanga. Evan's eyebrows drew together in a frown.

"We have taken up a collection," said Baba, pulling an envelope from his pocket. He opened it and spilled a few shillings into her hand.

Blessing felt happy to see that shiny money, made up of many small contributions.

But the real surprise followed. Blessing's eyes grew wide as Evan dug in his pocket, then stepped forward and added two shillings to the collection.

Evan wasn't usually generous with his allowance. Blessing smiled at him—maybe hearing about the "I Have a Dream" speech had really affected him—but Evan just squatted down, digging at the ground with a stick.

Mrs. Chinyanga stared at the coins, then wrapped them quickly in her handkerchief. "Thank you, Reverend. Please tell your congregation thank you." She said to Evan. "Thank you, young man."

Clutching his side and panting, Christopher returned with the biscuits and milk.

Albert helped Elizabeth bring the kettle out, then came back carrying a rusted tin tray with a bowl of sugar cubes; the milk, in a pitcher; the biscuits, spread on a plate; and a collection of china teacups, each one different.

Blessing squatted next to Evan. "Those children would like to eat biscuits too, but they just stand there watching us," he said.

Evan slipped a biscuit from the plate and held it out to Albert.

Albert put both hands behind his back. "It's for you," he said.

"You take it," urged Evan, offering the biscuit until Albert reached for it.

Elizabeth and Christopher looked at the ground.

"You too," Evan said, reaching for more.

Blessing had never seen Evan so generous! What was going on?

As Mrs. Chinyanga poured the tea, she said, "I'm worried about Gladman." Passing out the cups, she said, "I thought he'd be safe on the Mission."

Baba glanced at Evan, then said slowly, "In these times, no place is safe. I myself was taken for questioning."

"Whatever for, Reverend?" Mr. Chinyanga asked.

"The police thought I might know something about the killing of that white farmer. They are also concerned about an illegal handbill being circulated in the area. The handbill shows an African dressed as a soldier. He's holding a gun."

Blessing looked up at Baba. *An African soldier? A gun?* Baba's mouth was set tight.

Blessing noticed that Evan was now doodling lines and squiggles with the stick. What *was* going on with him?

Mr. Chinyanga frowned. Mrs. Chinyanga set her cup down so hard the tea sloshed.

A bus rattled by.

"The government will view this as treason," whispered Mrs. Chinyanga.

"That's the work of the freedom fighters," said Mr. Chinyanga. "May they free my brother and nephew!"

Evan put down the stick and sat cross-legged. First he'd handed out shillings and biscuits, and now he was acting so gloomy.

Blessing whispered, "Where's James Bond when we need him?" but Evan didn't smile.

"In any case," Baba said, "the police thought that because people confide in me, I might know something useful."

"And do you?" whispered Mrs. Chinyanga.

"If I did, I couldn't say. A pastor's conversations are private."

Blessing drank all of his tea in one gulp. What *did* Baba know? Did there come a time when those conversations shouldn't be kept private?

Albert brought out a car made of wire. Without looking at Blessing, he set it down. The car had shoe-polish tins for wheels, bottle caps for headlights, and a steering wheel made of wire and inner tubes.

"Caleb would love this car," Blessing said, holding it up so Evan could see.

Evan only glanced. Usually he'd hold out both hands for such a treasure.

Blessing studied the car, thinking of how to make one just like it. "Or I could make a wire airplane," he said.

"Hmm," Evan said, nodding slightly.

Was Evan getting a fever?

Albert moved the car in the dirt. He stopped it. He moved it and stopped it. "Now you," he said.

Blessing passed him a biscuit, then drove the toy car, making tracks in the swept dirt, still listening hard to the grown-ups. He'd heard talk of freedom fighters, but only talk. Now there was more than just talk. There was proof of treason.

Out

The Reverend Mudavanhu had launched into his sermon. A breeze from the nearby window lapped at his satin robes, then floated into the rest of the church.

Evan doodled aimlessly in his sketchbook. How was Mrs. Chinyanga going to pay the children's school fees? How long would her handkerchief of coins last? Was there a way he could send her more of his allowance without arousing suspicions? Mrs. Chinyanga didn't look like a Communist. He drew a hard line across the paper.

"Violence begets violence," the Reverend Mudavanhu was saying. "The forces of terror are building their arsenals among us. We must hold firm in our pacifism."

Evan hoped the Shumba were listening diligently but didn't dare lift his head to look.

All at once, the reverend stopped preaching.

Evan glanced up to see him staring at the back of the church. He, along with everyone else, turned to look.

It was Gladman, swaggering in. He had a fresh scar on his cheek. His arm hung in a sling. His crazy eyes swerved this way and that.

Gladman was out of jail.

At last the reverend said, "Welcome home, *mwanangu*."

Evan squeezed his eyes shut. Soft-boiled egg and toast rose into his throat. How had Gladman gotten free?

Had the police officers revealed their source?

"He's been *tortured*!" Blessing whispered.

"I'm not blind," Evan hissed. He could hardly keep from making a dash for the door by the altar. But that exit was too far, too obvious.

When the reverend continued his sermon, the Shumba spoke Shona so loud among themselves that Evan could hardly hear Mrs. Zezengwe.

People turned and glared. Burly Ford put his finger to his lips and hissed, "Shhh!"

But nothing would shush the Shumba.

"Why are you tapping your foot like that?" whispered Blessing.

Evan froze. No one must notice him. But he couldn't stop his heart's tremble.

He felt as see-through as a piece of glass. Surely everyone knew what he'd done. He wished that he could pray. But would God help him now?

At last, the Reverend Mudavanhu finished his sermon, uttered the final prayers, and blessed the whole congregation, including the noisy young men in the back.

Evan bowed his head, trying to receive the blessing, willing it to wash over him like a protective film.

From the back of the church came the sound of snarling.

People moved into the aisles to look.

Evan stood up on a pew, and after a moment, Blessing joined him.

A short-legged dog with a bare patch on its neck and another dog, this one with a curly tail, raced up to the altar. With ears flattened to the sides of their heads, they circled each other.

The curly-tailed dog dove forward, and the two dogs made one ball of growling fur. Grunts and yips filled the church.

Evan looked around. With the excitement, maybe he could make his getaway. He moved as though to climb down from the pew.

"Where are you going?" Blessing demanded.

It wouldn't work. He couldn't escape. "Nowhere," Evan replied.

The reverend, his robes getting tangled, and the albino— Tickey, with the yellow hair—kicked at the dogs. They tried to shoo them out.

Mai Sibanda aimed her toy rifle.

Short Legs yelped, and blood ran from the bare patch.

"Yeah, Curly Tail!" Blessing called.

The fight could almost make him forget, Evan thought.

Crazy Baba Sixpence threw a coat over Curly Tail and dragged him out. Short Legs lowered his tail and snuck off.

Mrs. Kasawira pulled on Evan's sleeve, then Blessing's. "Get down from the pew, boys!"

The Reverend Mudavanhu went back to the pulpit, straightening his robes. "How shamefully those dogs behave! Dear brothers and sisters, those dogs demonstrate why we humans must not fight among ourselves."

Evan heard the sound of barking outside. The dogs were at it again.

As the recessional played, Gladman led the Shumba out the front instead of through the doors leading back to the church hall and the tables of food.

Evan stood on tiptoe, watching the exodus.

There was a hubbub outside, as though all the Shumba were talking at once.

"Sounds like a riot," said Blessing.

People peeked through the front door; some ventured outside, eager to welcome Gladman home.

"Let's go see," said Blessing.

Evan eyed the door by the altar again. "I don't feel well," he said. "I ate something rotten."

Blessing looked him over, top to bottom.

Evan felt wretched in every atom of his body. Yet he'd call attention to himself if he left now.

He followed Blessing through the congregation until they found themselves part of the crowd gathered outside the church.

Gladman stood on a chair, his Shumba close.

The damp heat pressed on all sides. Evan fanned himself with his sketchbook.

Gladman lifted his good arm, and the crowd, especially the Shumba, grew quiet.

Gladman began to speak in Shona.

From somewhere in the back, Evan heard Mrs. Zezengwe's

soft voice begin the translation: "'Let me tell you a Bible story. A story of betrayal.'"

The missionaries moved closer to Mrs. Zezengwe. Evan scanned the crowd, looking for a quick way out.

"One night a trusted disciple of Jesus led a mob of men with lanterns, swords, and clubs," Gladman said. "This disciple went to Jesus and kissed him. That was the signal. 'Whomever I kiss, He is the One; seize Him.'" Gladman paused, his forehead glistening.

The crowd murmured.

Evan pressed his back against the pillar. His stomach churned wildly.

"And that disciple, brothers and sisters, that man, was Judas Iscariot." Gladman wiped his face with a bloodstained handkerchief.

People looked at each other and murmured again. Some of the younger boys worked their way closer to the Shumba.

Evan lowered his eyes. If he concentrated on the concrete underfoot, he might get through this. He didn't want to see Gladman's bruises, that broken arm. He swatted at a mosquito.

"For thirty pieces of silver, Judas betrayed the Son of God," said Gladman.

Blessing reached for the mosquito and clapped his hands. "Got it," he muttered, shaking his hand until the squashed mosquito dropped off.

"There is a Judas among us. One of you betrayed me."

As Gladman turned his gaze—one eye on the crowd, the other swimming away—Evan looked into the sky.

Finally, Gladman said, too quietly, "The police couldn't prove their case. They had to let me go. So someone will have to try again to betray the cause of African liberation. If that someone is one of you, let him deliver his kiss."

Evan bit his lip.

Again, Gladman turned his head, this time as though offering one cheek, then the other. "Deliver your kiss," he repeated. He looked over the crowd once more, one eye fixed on the congregation.

Evan found himself staring into the crazy eye. It focused straight on him. He was sure of that.

Gladman motioned for those crowding around his chair to move back. He seemed about to step down.

Evan moved back, bumping into a pillar.

But then Gladman stood tall again, saying softly, "When the whites took control, they outlawed ironworking. They were afraid we'd make guns. Now friendly countries are giving us weapons. We shall take back the land that was stolen from us!"

People looked at one another. Some nodded. Others shook their heads and muttered.

Evan's stomach churned. His knees trembled.

Gladman jumped down and was surrounded by the Shumba.

The crowd broke up, moving toward the church hall and lunch.

Guns and Peaches

"Let's not go to the end of the line this time," Blessing said as they headed toward the church hall.

"I'm not hungry, anyway," Evan said.

Inside, Blessing scooted in and out between clumps of people. Finally, he arrived at the table spread with the potluck lunch.

Flies had discovered the food, and Mrs. Mudiwa stood guard, waving them off.

As Blessing took lunch, he dug underneath to avoid the bits a fly might have landed on.

The missionaries, including Evan's parents, instead of spreading out among the Africans, grouped together. They whispered among themselves, their eyes avoiding the Shumba.

The Shumba didn't whisper but spoke loudly in Shona.

Baba sat at a table with the African teachers.

Blessing sat down next to Evan, who'd taken nothing to eat.

"What are they saying?" Evan asked. His cheeks were flushed pink, and his damp hair stuck to his forehead.

"They're talking about joining the *vakomana*, the freedom fighters in the bush." Blessing himself was beginning to have a queasy stomach. The violence Baba preached against had come into the church hall.

"Now what are they talking about?"

"Judas."

Evan dropped his fountain pen and scrambled to pick it up.

Gladman talked the loudest, lifting his good arm up, swinging the bad one in the sling.

He was no longer the meek leader of the Bible-study group. He was talking like the leader of a revolution. Blessing thought of Gladman's poor, struggling mother. She just needed her son to behave himself and help the family get by.

Instead of eating, Baba kept his eyes on the Shumba.

"Translate," Evan begged.

Blessing set his empty plate on the floor. "Gladman says that in his cartoons, Mr. Deaton always draws us Africans as helpless victims. For example, there's the one where elephants are trampling us like soft blades of grass. We should be sharp blades of steel instead, cutting the feet of the elephants so they fall. We must be victors, not victims, he says." As he spoke, Blessing felt the awful power of these harsh, forbidden words. He hoped Evan would be satisfied and not want to hear more.

The Shumba gave a cheer.

Gladman sat down, and Baba walked toward him. Baba stood over the Shumba, his white pastoral collar gleaming against his skin.

"Keep translating," Evan said.

Blessing drew a deep breath and echoed Baba's voice: "'If we gain our freedom with guns, as you suggest, Gladman, one day our leaders will hold their power with guns. I pray that we attain majority rule by peaceful means. In any case, leave these decisions to the adults. Let these children continue their studies.'"

Baba waved his hand at the high-school boys.

Gladman gave a tiny nod. Tough as he was, he was no match for Baba.

Everyone respected Baba. Everyone knew that, no matter how upset Baba was, he would always stand by his congregation. He would never turn against anyone.

After Baba went back to his seat and his plate of food, the young men kept talking, but now in whispers. But, though they now spoke softly, the words were the same. Gladman forked up big bites of food and swallowed without chewing.

Evan was breathing as though he'd just played a game of football.

Blessing looked around at the missionaries. They ate in silence, faster than usual, their silverware clicking against the plates.

Evan still ate nothing at all.

If the missionaries understood the Shumba's Shona talk, they might leave Rhodesia, Blessing thought. They'd be disappointed that their hard work toward peace had come to so little. Would Africans, even those on the Mission, really take up arms against white people?

The missionaries wouldn't feel safe here anymore.

Why had the messages of Jesus and the Reverend King and Mahatma Gandhi not reached Gladman and his Shumba?

◆ ◆ ◆

After lunch, the boys played football as usual, including members of the Shumba.

"I don't feel like playing," Evan announced.

"Then I don't either," said Blessing, and they sat on the grass and watched.

The other boys kept picking green peaches from the nearby peach tree. They took one bite before throwing them down.

From the doorway of the church hall, Mr. Ford surveyed the scene. "You're wasting good fruit!" he finally shouted.

"What do you mean?" Petrol asked.

"You can only eat peaches that are on the ground!" Mr. Ford said. "Only the fallen ones are ripe."

Blessing stared at Mr. Ford. If he only knew of the threatening words spoken at lunch. He couldn't help thinking that if anyone did get violent, Mr. Ford might be one of the victims.

Kingsize looked at Mr. Ford, then hurled the tennis ball hard against the tree. "Oh, look!" he said. "Some fruit has fallen!"

Everyone laughed, then ran to grab fallen peaches.

Mr. Ford put his hands on his fat hips and scowled.

Tshombe!

That night, while Dad and Mom were at a missionary meeting, Evan heard shouting from the hill above the house. He closed his book and listened. Nighttime at the Mission was normally so peaceful that you could hear the whir of every insect.

Could the noise be the wind? Branches thrashed against the windows. But, no—Evan listened carefully—it was human cries.

He closed both hands around his book. Did people know that he was the Judas? Was a mob on the way to get him?

Or were they only scaring away a troop of baboons? Had someone seen a leopard?

He stood up, his heart dancing. If they came for him, he could hide under the bed. He could arm himself with the tennis racket.

Should he hide the bronze star, his cadet medal?

But the cries remained distant.

Evan crept down the hallway. Inside, the clock ticked predictably. But outside . . . outside, the night twirled and snapped, a chaos of wind and noise.

The doorknob was slick under his hand. He turned it, swung the door open, and found himself on the *stoep*.

Cool air floated around his ankles. Starlight shone on a world torn by wind.

A crowd of shouting people ran down the road. Evan climbed onto the *stoep* railing to get a better view. What on earth was happening?

He jumped down from the railing, descended the steps, and crossed the grass to the road.

The wind gusted so hard that the blue-gum trees rocked. Even the stars trembled.

Evan saw Kingsize, Lovemore, Petrol, and other members of the Shumba stuffing their pockets with small rocks.

He stepped back. He clenched his fists and positioned himself out of the boys' sight, close to the trunk of a custard-apple tree. The fallen fruit squished under his shoes, releasing a sweet, decaying scent.

For a moment, the crowd parted, and Evan glimpsed the African teachers standing in a line, holding the crowd back.

Gladman Chinyanga raised his good arm, the hand making a fist.

"There's a Judas Iscariot on this mission!" someone shouted.

"Go home!" yelled Mrs. Matondo.

The wind roared and more custard apples fell, splattering at Evan's feet.

"Judas! Judas! Who are you?" the crowd chanted.

Some of the students held up large stones.

"Go home!" another teacher pleaded. "You won't solve anything like this!"

Evan shook like the leaves of the blue-gum trees above. The Shumba were looking for him!

Someone threw a custard apple. Someone else screamed.

Evan braced himself against the trunk of the tree. He looked to the stars to steady himself. But in the clear black, they glittered and winked and couldn't be trusted.

Something landed with a dull thud. A stone?

The crowd exploded like a thunderhead releasing its fury. To shouts of "*Tshombe!* Traitor!" people pushed and elbowed their neighbors.

Evan heard glass breaking far off in the distance.

Seconds later, he heard shattering close by—the window of Burly Ford's house.

The crowd roared.

"Someone betrayed us, *mufundisi.* Gladman Chinyanga knows!"

"There's a *tshombe* in our midst!"

Someone grabbed Evan by the arm. In the dark, he made out Grace's round face. "Evan!" She brought her lips to his ear. "You have to get out of here!"

Evan saw Dad running toward them. He put his arm around Evan and pulled him in tight. "What's this all about, Grace?"

"I'm not sure, Mr. Campbell. But it may not be safe here for white people."

Dad seized Evan by the hand, then Grace. "Let's go!" he ordered, hurrying them toward the house.

As they crossed the *stoep*, the floorboards thundered with their footsteps. Dad swung open the door.

The house was still dark inside. When Evan reached for the light switch, Dad grabbed his wrist. "No lights tonight, Evan."

"What is it?" Mom came into the hallway, a shadowy figure.

"Some of the African students are up in arms. Evan was out there."

"Oh, no," said Mom. "Evan." As she folded him close, he smelled the talc she used in the heat.

The shaking inside him slowly stilled, but outside, the shouts continued.

"Pack your things, Evan," Dad said.

In his dark room, Evan pulled open drawers. He felt for underwear and socks. He felt for his school uniform on the hanger, then reached to the back of his closet, where he kept his cadet uniform hidden. He fingered the bronze star on the pocket of the shirt, then jerked the shirt off the hanger and laid it in the suitcase.

He should confess to Mom and Dad. He had to tell someone before he burst with the secret.

In the hallway, Evan heard Mom and Dad murmuring. Dad cranked the handle of the black telephone on the wall. Silence. Dad replaced the receiver with a clunk. "No operator," he said.

"We'll have to go unannounced," Mom said.

"Stay in the house, Grace," Dad said. "Lock the doors."

He came into Evan's room. "It's time."

Evan followed Dad down the dark hallway.

Behind them, Mom said, "Start the car, then we'll run out."

Evan and Mom listened at the side door—cracked just a hair—while Dad climbed into the station wagon. He shut the door quietly.

"Let's hope the car cooperates," Mom breathed.

But of course it didn't. Dad tried, waited, tried again.

"He's rushing," said Mom. "He's flooding the engine."

"Not now . . ." Evan muttered.

When the car was finally idling, Mom opened the door wide. "Go!" she ordered.

Evan dashed out and climbed in, followed by Mom. They jammed down the door locks, and Mom began to recite the Lord's Prayer. As she begged God for protection, her voice high and faltering, the words reminded Evan of shattered glass.

River of Blood

Everyone was looking forward to watching Lovemore practice dancing with Nyasha.

"Maybe he'll fall in love for real," said Wastetime.

"And they'll kiss right onstage," Rishon said.

"Not a chance," said Blessing.

But, even though it was already dark, neither Lovemore nor Nyasha had come. Not any of the older boys or girls were there.

Blessing wondered if their absence had anything to do with the talk at lunch.

Mrs. Gainsby looked at her watch. "We'd better go ahead without them. Let's rehearse the train-station scene."

The little ones gathered.

Blessing waved to Caleb. He made a gesture as though pulling a zipper across his lips.

Just as Mrs. Bloomquist played the opening notes, there was the sound of crashing and shouting.

Somewhere close, glass broke.

"Dear Lord," said Mrs. Gainsby, shifting her big body back and forth.

Blessing rushed across the stage to Caleb, taking him by the arm.

Mrs. Bloomquist stood up, her hand on her mouth as if she were holding in a scream.

"Oh my, oh my," said Mrs. Gainsby.

Mrs. Bloomquist ran onto the stage, her long Swedish legs going two steps at a time. "Attention, older boys and girls! Get your little brothers and sisters and take them home. Little ones with no siblings will go with Mrs. Gainsby."

Onstage, children ran every which way. Some cried. More glass shattered.

Mrs. Bloomquist returned to the piano and quietly played a tune from *Oklahoma!* about the sun and rain.

"Blessing!" Caleb cried. "Blessing!"

"I'm taking you home, *mununʼuna.*"

A window right there in Beit Hall shattered.

Everyone ran out the back door, shoving and screaming.

Outside, a line of headlights punctuated the darkness. When a Land Rover pulled close, Blessing saw the government lion again: police from Umtali! He pulled Caleb off the road.

"Let's go see," said Caleb, peeking from the bush.

"We should go home."

"But I want to *see.*"

Blessing wanted to see too. He looked down the road toward home, then toward the red taillights of the convoy. "Okay, but we'll have to be careful." He hoisted Caleb up and carried him piggyback. He ran into the Land Rovers' diesel fumes, which thickened the black night.

The convoy had stopped by the printing press, where a big wild group had gathered. The police got out, slamming the doors, lifting their clubs high.

Caleb squeezed Blessing's hand.

James Zezengwe picked up a rock.

"No, James!" shouted Caleb.

But James threw the rock, and a storm of shards flew in all directions.

A police officer raised his club high and hit James on the shoulder. He fell, rolling along the ground.

Blessing jerked hard, as though he'd been the one hit.

Then another got clubbed.

"He's hurt!" Caleb cried, burying his face in Blessing's shirt.

James got up. He and three other big boys charged the officers.

An officer fired a shot in the air. Everyone screamed and ran.

Suddenly Caleb screamed and fell down. "My foot! My foot, Blessing!" he shouted.

Blessing bent down, felt the sole of Caleb's foot, and pulled out a big piece of glass. A hot river poured into his hands.

Up Caleb went, piggyback again. Blessing ran and ran to the infirmary, which he hoped was still there and not wrecked and broken, while Caleb's blood ran hot on his wrists.

Exodus

As they drove through the darkness of the Mission, Evan heard the sounds of breaking glass. Figures ran through the darkness. He lay down, hiding his face against the seat.

Mom was still praying. She hadn't stopped once since they'd gotten into the car—"Our Father, who art in heaven . . ."—and by her muffled voice, Evan knew that she too was lying low.

"Where are we going?" Evan mumbled, tilting his mouth to the side.

"To the Cherrymans'," Dad answered. "You'll be safe there."

"But Cyril and I aren't friends anymore."

"Doesn't matter," said Dad.

Evan shivered. His shoes smelled of rotting custard apples. When the car turned, he lifted himself up and saw that they'd passed through the Mission gates and were sailing safely down the main road.

"The police have just arrived," said Dad. "A whole convoy."

"Goodness gracious," Mom said. "How shameful to have our mission out of control."

Dad drummed his fingers on the steering wheel. "Gladman should have stayed in jail."

"George!" Mom protested.

"Now he's got everyone worked up."

Evan leaned his head on his suitcase. He was like a wild animal rescued from the Kariba Dam. Like an animal being taken onto Noah's Ark during the Great Flood. Rescued from the rising flood of violence.

But he was no innocent animal.

He was suddenly exhausted, as though every bit of him had been wrung out.

When the car stopped, Evan woke to see Cyril's brick house, square and solid in the dark night.

Dad marched down the path to rap on the front door. The verandah light clicked on, and Mr. Cherryman opened up. His bulky shape filled the doorway, almost hiding Mrs. Cherryman behind him, her head a mass of curlers.

Dad turned and beckoned.

Evan yanked his suitcase from the backseat and followed Mom. In the dim light, throaty hibiscus bloomed along the path. Roses dropped petals on the stepping stones, and insects hurled themselves against the screens.

"Evan will be safe with us," Mrs. Cherryman was saying. "Not to worry. You and Phyllis take care of yourselves."

Evan clasped his hands in front of him. Everything was topsy-turvy. Here he was, taking refuge with other whites, with a classmate who'd turned against him. Refuge from the Africans, who'd been friends. He'd become their betrayer, a Judas.

He'd even betrayed Blessing.

Kaffir lover, he thought.

Cyril came out of his room, dressed in pajamas, his hair mussed. "What're you doing here, Cowboy?"

"Nothing."

"How can it be nothing when you've ridden all this way in the night? Look. My boy's bringing you a bed."

A gray-haired African had appeared with a sleeping cot, carrying it down the hall to Cyril's room.

"That's no boy," Evan couldn't help but say. "That man could be your grandfather."

"Okay, sorry," Cyril said. "I forgot."

"Good-bye, hon," said Mom, pulling Evan tight against her for a moment.

Dad laid a hand on his shoulder. "Everything's going to be fine. Now, get to bed."

"Come on," said Cyril, opening the door to his room.

When they were in bed, Cyril said, "Are you here because of that terr you turned in?"

Evan shifted, and the cot squeaked. He'd almost forgotten that Cyril knew. He was glad of the gauze of his mosquito netting, separating them; but, of all people, Cyril might now be his ally. "I am," he finally said.

"You did the right thing," Cyril said.

"Hmm." Evan felt a rush of gratitude. "There's trouble on the Mission right now, and it's all my fault."

He heard Cyril sit up, his bed groaning a little. "What do you mean, 'trouble'?"

"People are angry."

"What are they doing?"

"Throwing rocks and custard apples. Breaking windows. Someone might even get shot."

"Shot? They have guns?" Cyril's bed groaned louder. "Who's shooting?"

"The police might be."

"All because of what you did?"

"I don't want to talk about it."

"Come on. . . ."

"No."

The room went silent. Evan heard the Cherrymans whispering in the hall. He rolled onto his side.

"Tomorrow we can sail my little boat," Cyril said at last.

"Sounds good."

"Know any new ghost stories?"

"Only the one about the hand with the oozing green pus," Evan answered.

"I've already heard that one."

"I'll think of another by tomorrow night."

"Catch some *Zs*, then."

"You too," Evan responded.

He lay awake, his mind twisting this way and that. He couldn't sleep for the smell of himself. He still reeked of rotten custard apples.

"Oh, Lord . . ."

The next morning, as Mai set down plates of white bread and margarine, Blessing asked, "Did you hear from the infirmary?"

"Caleb's doing fine. Baba checked on him late last night."

"He stopped bleeding?"

"Yes, finally." Mai returned with a pot of tea and a cup, placing them near the bread.

"Has anyone heard from Evan? Does anyone know where he was last night?" He hoped Evan hadn't gotten hurt in the riot like Caleb.

"The Campbells took Evan into Umtali. He's staying with a classmate."

"He's okay, then?"

"Seems to be."

Blessing spread the creamy yellow margarine. So, Evan was parked safely at a white boy's house. As Blessing took a bite of bread, he thought of the games the two boys must be playing, the nice food they were probably eating. Evan wasn't here at the Mission, helping to clean up. He wasn't here waiting for whatever might come next. He wasn't worrying his head off over Caleb's cut foot.

Blessing poured tea into his cup. He shouldn't think unkindly of Evan. He should be glad he was safe. After all, just a moment ago, he'd been hoping he was out of harm's way.

After school, Blessing went up the steps of the infirmary, between people waiting in the shade of a lucky-bean tree. His feet felt like two heavy stones.

Everywhere he heard the scratch of raking and the tinkling sound of glass being dumped into bins.

He'd learned that *Oklahoma!* had been canceled. The windows of Beit Hall had been broken, and Mrs. Gainsby was so fed up with the Shumba's wrecking the Mission that she and her husband were going home to England. And Lovemore, who played Curly, had been knocked down in a stampede, his mouth now too smashed to talk.

Blessing entered the infirmary, with its polished floors smelling of Sunshine wax, the many doors leading into the sickrooms.

"Hello, Blessing," said Grace's sister, Prudence, getting up from her desk. "Caleb's just woken up."

As Blessing followed Prudence down the hallway, her dark-blue nurse uniform whispered.

On the walls hung a chart of the human body and posters about malaria and bilharzia, instructions on how to dig a pit latrine and how to treat a snakebite. But nothing about protecting one's little brother from an angry crowd.

Prudence opened a door, and there was Caleb, lying on an iron bed. His foot was raised high, wrapped in a big bandage.

"Blessing!" He held out his little arms.

Blessing gave him a big hug. "You'll be fine soon, *mununʼuna.* You'll be running again soon, *mununʼuna.* You'll see."

From his pocket he brought out maize stalks, elephant grass, and leaves.

As he made Caleb's airplane, he whispered, "Your foot will heal. You will be all better soon. You'll run and fly this plane. You'll see."

That night, the Land Rover came again for Baba.

This time, the police didn't speak to Baba. They merely opened the door of the Land Rover and gestured.

Blessing stood with Mai and Mbuya in the yard, watching. As the Land Rover drove off, he silently recited all the Psalms he knew: *"For thy rod and thy staff shall comfort me. . . ." "Thou hast made the earth to tremble. . . ."*

That night, Blessing listened for the soft closing of the front door. But there was no shush of a door opening, no soft click.

"Why is your father still away?" Mrs. Zezengwe asked Blessing as she tended the blue lilies of the Nile and magenta-colored zinnias on the altar.

"Maybe they think he knows something about the riot," he answered, pausing from his job of sweeping the sanctuary.

"Maybe they think he started it," Mrs. Mudiwa whispered as she picked up a fallen zinnia.

"Ha!" Mrs. Zezengwe waved her hand. "How could they think that? Every Sunday, he preaches against violence."

"Might he have turned someone in, then? Did the reverend turn in Gladman? Could Gladman"—Mrs. Mudiwa lowered her voice even more—"be one of the killers?"

"Even if he is, my baba would never betray a fellow African," said Blessing, moving the broom in a long, firm arc.

Every afternoon Blessing waited by the road for the police Land Rover to bring Baba back. A rat was eating his heart. "Oh, Lord, hear my prayer. . . ." Even the *mupuranga* trees prayed.

What if Baba never came back? Blessing had heard of families whose loved ones had disappeared forever. But that couldn't happen to Baba. Whenever the thought arose, Blessing put his foot on a round *mupuranga* pod, twisting his heel hard until the seed popped.

Waiting, he rode his bike in circles. He paced the red dirt road.

He wished Evan were here to wait with him. But Evan still hadn't returned. He was gone, but at least he wasn't in jail.

On the third evening, Blessing was throwing stones at tree trunks, when he looked up to see a tiny person walking through the Mission gates. He squinted. Surely Baba wouldn't be *walking* home.

But as the figure grew larger, Blessing recognized the slightly uneven gait.

It *was* Baba! It was!

Blessing called toward the house: "Mai!" But he couldn't wait for her.

He ran to meet Baba, his legs burning, his heart singing: *Hallelujah! Hallelujah! Jesus has listened! Baba is home!*

Homecoming

In art, Evan was carving his leopard on the block of linoleum. The body and leafy background were done now. He had only the head, tail, and legs to complete.

Behind him, he heard boys whispering.

"Campbell's staying at Cherryman's," said Johan.

"Mmm," murmured Graham. "He ratted on that kaffir. Someone probably found out. And now the kaffir's out of jail and Campbell's in a bloody mess."

"He'll never go back to the Mission, eh?" said Adrian.

Evan carved more slowly.

"Guess he's not a kaffir lover, after all," Johan said.

"He's a *kaffir hater.*"

Giggles.

Evan's guts twisted. He put a hand to his belly. He put a hand to the cadet medal hanging from his pocket.

"Leave Cowboy alone," said Cyril, who was sitting behind Evan.

Without turning around, Evan smiled.

"I could make up a story and get a medal too," said Graham.

"He *made it up*?"

"Must have. They wouldn't have let the *munt* out otherwise."

Evan clenched his jaw. With the sharp linoleum knife, he dug out the leopard's leg. He dug too deep and severed the leg from the body.

"Rollins should take the medal back, then. Let someone else have it."

At that, Evan turned around and faced the boys. "I didn't do it for the medal. I did it to fight Communism!"

They snorted.

Graham held up his curved linoleum knife. "Here's my sickle. Turn me in!"

Just as the afternoon storm struck with a rumble of thunder, Evan plunged his own knife deep into the leopard's neck. Water hit the windows sideways, plastering bright bougainvillea flowers to the glass.

"Shut up, all of you!" said Cyril.

"Yeah, shut up," Evan echoed. But when no one was looking, he unpinned the medal and held it clenched in his fist. The sharp points of the star bit into his fingers.

After school on Friday, the plum-colored station wagon stood idling at the curb. "The coast is clear," sang out Mom through the open window. "I'm taking you home!"

Evan glanced at the rugby players, shouting and scrambling on the field.

"Why are you dragging your feet, hon? If you're worried about the Mission, don't be. All is calm."

Mrs. Cherryman pulled up in her maroon Morris Minor.

"Thank you for having Evan," Mom said, getting out of the station wagon. She extended a hand to Mrs. Cherryman.

"Your boy was a pleasure."

Cyril came to stand with them, his school hat tipped back on his head.

"Evan's mum is here to take him home, dear," said Mrs. Cherryman.

"Cheerio, then," Cyril said.

"Cheerio," said Evan, lifting a hand. "See you at school."

During the week, they'd sailed the miniature sailboat, looked at paintings of the American Revolution, read stacks of comics, and even trekked into the bush behind Cyril's house in search of the leopard.

Now Evan had to head back to the grim reality of the Mission. The thought of seeing Blessing was the only bright note. And yet all was so tangled. . . .

Mrs. Cherryman tilted her face to the gloomy sky. "We'd all best head home before this storm hits."

"Yes, let's do hurry," said Mom, walking toward the car.

Evan lifted his hand once more in good-bye.

"Cheerio," Cyril repeated.

Starting the engine, Mom said, "The Cherrymans were good to keep you."

"Um-hum," Evan said. "What's been happening at home?"

Mom had called him once that week, but due to a storm, the line had gone dead.

"The night of the riot, the police stood outside our house protecting us." Mom laughed a little. "We didn't really need them. We would have been fine."

"Did the riot go on a long time?"

"It was over with by the time we got back from the Cherrymans'."

As they passed the turnoff for Cyril's, Evan pressed his forehead to the cool window.

"The vandalism was certainly disheartening for the missionaries and the African teachers alike," Mom said. "The students broke windows all over the Mission. They went on an absolute rampage."

A rampage. Evan shut his eyes.

He should tell Mom everything. He should make her turn the car around. He should stay at Cyril's forever.

Leaves blew along the road as clouds moved in.

"How's Blessing?"

Mom sighed. "The police took his father away again. This time for three whole days. The family was fit to be tied."

"Why would they take the *reverend*?" Evan sat up tall, every muscle alert.

"Probably because of the riot. There are rumors that it was started not only by Gladman but also by the men who've been running away to the bush."

Evan knit his fingers together, first one way, then the other.

"And Blessing's little brother got injured that awful night."

"*Caleb?* What happened? How bad is he?"

"He stepped on broken glass and cut his foot. He bled quite a bit."

Evan clenched his hands hard. How could things get any worse? His friend would rather die than see his little brother hurt.

"Drive faster, Mom. I have to find Blessing!" Evan leaned on the dashboard, inches closer to the Mission. "I have to see him right away!"

Blessing was his *sahwira,* he thought for the very first time. *My* sahwira, he thought, his heart beating like a beast in his chest.

The car crested Christmas Pass and coasted down into the valley. The Mission lay below like a collection of innocent toy buildings.

"By the way," Mom said, "Gladman disappeared during the riot. Because he was said to be the instigator, the police were eager to find him. Rumor has it that he escaped over the border."

"He's gone, then?"

"For now, anyway."

At least there was something to be thankful for. Evan leaned back in the seat. But he kept his hands locked.

Already he saw the bishop birds over the river. They were almost there—every turn of the tires brought him closer.

As Mom drove through the gate into the Mission, Evan saw angry-looking shards littering the ground around the buildings. He saw crews of students sweeping.

"It's taking days to clean up all the damage," Mom said.

Evan squeezed his eyes shut, opening them only when he felt the car turn into the driveway.

"I'll be home by dinner," Evan said, climbing out. He tore off his school tie and flung it on the seat.

Mom looked at the clouds, now curdled into a dark mass. "Don't stay out that long. Quite a storm is brewing."

Silver Flashes

As the storm lunged across the sky, Blessing hurried toward home. Leaving the school grounds, he saw Evan going up the road on his bike. "Hey!" he called out. "You've been gone so long!"

Thunder cracked. Beyond the baby fold, where the orphans lived, lightning shot down.

Blessing ran under a large tree.

Evan had turned around. He was coming back. At the bend of the road, he shouted, "How's Caleb?"

"Out of the infirmary!" Blessing shouted back.

Evan skidded close and jumped off the bike.

"But *Oklahoma!* is canceled, and Mr. and Mrs. Gainsby are leaving for England," said Blessing.

"Oh, no!" Evan cried.

The wind rose and the sky got blacker. Blessing shivered. "I'm glad you're home."

Evan rang his bike bell, a bright little sound in the snarl of the approaching storm. "Me too."

"Why, look who we have here," a voice close by said.

Blessing turned to see Petrol, Kingsize, and Lovemore standing on the edge of the road. Lovemore, with his smashed mouth. Blessing jerked his cardboard suitcase of school books across his chest.

"Bhunu and Blessing," said Lovemore, his words coming out like he'd chewed them.

"We have unfinished business with you, Blessing," said Kingsize.

They moved forward.

"Your *baba*'s spent time with the police lately," said Petrol. "We think your *baba* got Gladman arrested."

Even though Evan had both feet on the ground, his bike wobbled. His mouth dropped open.

"Baba?" was all Blessing could say. However had they gotten *that* idea?

"In fact, we *know* it," Petrol said, and laughed. "Gladman told your *baba* something, and the reverend broke his pastoral promise of secrecy."

They came closer. Closer than a bike length. Blessing shrank back against the trunk of the tree.

Thunder again.

A big flash silvered everything, showing up the blade in Petrol's hand. Was it really a knife? Were the boys that serious?

Blessing threw his suitcase toward Evan. The latch broke, and the books skidded out. "Run, Evan! Run get help!" he shouted.

Evan acted as if he hadn't noticed the heavy suitcase landing near him. He just stood holding on to the handlebars of his bike. Hadn't he heard the words? Didn't he understand what might happen?

Suddenly, Evan dropped the bike—it shuddered to the ground—and took three steps, to stand between Blessing and the boys. He lifted his chin. "*I* did it," he announced against the wind. "It wasn't the reverend."

Thunder cracked.

"Can't hear you, Bhunu," Lovemore yelled.

Evan stepped even closer. "I got Gladman arrested," he shouted. "I was the one."

"You?" Blessing cried. *"You? What for?"*

The first big drops of rain fell.

Between one thunderclap and the next, Blessing watched the boys move in on Evan. Like lightning. They raised their fists, Petrol his knife.

Blessing stepped forward. What could he do? There were three of them. They were big. . . .

Petrol whistled the *Oklahoma!* tune about a golden meadow.

"Ndokurowa!" yelled Kingsize.

Blessing ran forward and grabbed Evan's bike. He lifted it up, the tires bouncing on the dirt, and swung his leg over.

The rain crashed. Gray, thick, heavy.

Blessing pedaled close to Evan, staying on the far side of the Shumba. "Let's go! Get on and let's go!"

Evan's light eyes grew so wide the white rims showed, then he flew to the bike and hopped on.

Blessing rode him out of there, his heart thudding like thunder, his blood flashing like lightning. Through the rain plunging down like tiny knives, he rode them both to safety.

Soul Force

Gusts of rain knocked the bike sideways. Evan held on tightly as Blessing pedaled along the muddy road.

Sometimes he thought he heard shouts, but when he looked back, there was only the thick wall of rain.

He'd had to confess. He couldn't let those boys hurt Blessing.

Flashes of lightning showed everything and nothing. Somewhere out there lay the red pond, with the raft at the bottom; the line of blue-gum trees along the red road; the red-roofed church and the baby fold.

At last they reached Evan's back door, the downpour drumming on the tin roof.

Blessing parked by the steps and slipped off, holding the bike steady. As Evan began to dismount, Blessing brought his face so close that Evan saw the tiny chip in his front tooth. "So *you* were the Judas?" The question unfurled into the wild air.

"I was," Evan said, shaking water from his face. "I did it." How could he explain, with this pummeling rain? How could he ever explain?

Just then, his tall sock caught on the bicycle chain. The bike fell, pushing him down. It hurt when the kickstand hit his leg, but the pain felt almost good.

In fact, he wished he could stay there in the mud, his face covered by the spinning wheel. He'd come to the worst thing now, worse even than being assaulted by the Shumba or mocked by classmates. His best friend now knew what he'd done.

"People are saying my *baba* was the traitor. But it was *you*!" Blessing cried. "You, Evan! Why?"

The back door swung open. "Why are you boys out there in this storm?" Grace exclaimed. "Blessing! Get Evan out from under that bicycle and come inside!"

Blessing lifted the bike.

Evan rolled up without meeting Blessing's eyes.

As they dove into the kitchen, Grace threw down a stack of newspapers. "Now, don't drip on the clean floor!"

They stepped onto the paper, so close that their elbows touched, their clothes plastered to their skin. Evan's knees shook, and his teeth chattered.

"What's happened to you two?" Mom asked, holding a paring knife. "You look like death warmed over." Behind her, potatoes rested on a cutting board.

Evan put a hand on his belly, catching his breath. "Something important," he finally managed.

"You're building a tree house? A fort?"

"Not that." Evan lifted his chin. "Something even more important. Everyone's wondering who turned in Gladman." He took a breath. "*I* did. I was fighting Communism." The words chugged into the steamy air of the kitchen.

Mom's knife clattered to the floor.

"Gladman's a Communist." Evan felt Blessing's breath quicken beside him. "I saw him printing the handbill the CID showed us that night. The Communist handbill."

Grace didn't bend to pick up the knife but stared at Evan.

He looked down at his feet, his cheeks hot. What must Grace think of him? And Mom? Was she proud or not? Did they see him as a warrior against Communism or as a Judas Iscariot? And Blessing. Would Blessing still call him a traitor, now that he'd heard about fighting Communists?

The cadet medal was in the pocket of his trousers, a weighty little reminder. Evan felt shame like a sticky crust on his skin.

Down the hall, the clock ticked, measuring time, sorting right from wrong.

"And just now I told some members of Gladman's Shumba what I've done," Evan added.

The clock struck the hour, the cuckoo bird sailing out as though it were a normal afternoon.

When the chiming ended, Mom said, "If those Shumba boys know, we'll have to get you out of here right now, Evan. They might start another riot."

Evan swallowed hard.

Mom looked at the pile of potatoes. She laid her hand on one, as if to test its size, its realness. Then she untied her checkered apron and threw it on the counter. "I wish your dad were here. But let's go."

Evan thought of how the Shumba had approached him in the rain. Would they come right into his house? Would they do that to a missionary family? He eyed the small knife, still on the floor.

By now the Shumba might be trying to find Gladman. Had he come back from Mozambique? By now Gladman might have told the people with the guns that he, Evan, was the *tshombe.*

Mom pulled the curtain across the window. "Lock the front door, Grace."

Evan gazed down at the wet newspaper. The headline read: RHODESIA VERSUS NEW ZEALAND CRICKET FINALS. "Thanks for saving me from the Shumba," he said, turning to Blessing.

Blessing shrugged.

A lump the size of a mango seed rose in Evan's throat. "I'll be back soon," he said, swallowing hard. "We'll build another raft."

Blessing shrugged again. Was he also focusing on the headlines?

Evan swiveled the toe of his shoe against the wet newspaper, digging a hole.

"Come," Mom beckoned as Grace returned from locking the front door. She drew all three of them into a hug.

Each looped an arm across the other's shoulders.

Grace began to cry.

Evan squeezed his eyes tight against the wall of tears. He'd have to leave the Mission. Maybe he'd even have to leave Africa, go back to the States.

Would this rain never stop?

"May the Lord keep us and bless us. In His name, amen." Mom's whisper was soft.

They broke apart. Evan felt himself separate again, alone.

"Will *you* be all right, Blessing?" Mom asked. "Will they come after you?"

"Not me, Mrs. Campbell. It's not me they care about now."

"Praise be, Blessing." Mom briefly took his hand. Then she picked up her purse and the car keys from the counter.

"I'm sorry, Blessing," Evan said as Mom took him by the arm and steered him out the door and into the drenching rain.

Following Mom, who was holding her purse over her head, keeping her curls dry, Evan sloshed through the puddles. They climbed inside the car, slamming the doors against the rain, against unseen dangers.

Blessing came outside and stood with his arms at his sides, the rain cascading over his dark shape.

Evan waved to him with one hand, wiping the steam off the window with the other.

Mom turned the key in the ignition once, then again, before the car growled to life.

As they drove away, Evan felt like one of the blue-gum trees, a gray form lashed by rain and wind. "I'm sorry, Mom."

"Everything will be fine, hon," she said.

"How?" he asked. "How can it be?"

Mom didn't answer.

They drove down the road, the rain almost hiding the turnoffs for the church and for Blessing's house. It fell in a thundering curtain over the bright-green football fields.

Close to the Mission gates, storm water flowed down a dip in the road. Mom stopped and leaned closer to the windshield. "Should I risk it?" she asked. The diamond of her wedding ring flashed warnings in the gloom.

Evan took a long look. The water wasn't really deep, but lately the station wagon had been temperamental. "There's no other way out," he said.

Little by little, Mom eased the car into the muddy red sea. The station wagon coughed, shuddered, and finally stalled.

Mom slapped the steering wheel, then laid her forehead against it. "I shouldn't have tried it."

"Old rust bucket," Evan said, stamping his foot on the floorboard. He tried to look out the steamed-up back window. Was anyone after them? Could bullets pass through glass? "Try again," he said.

Mom turned the key, but the engine made no sound. Not even a hint of a whisper. "Now what?" she said.

Evan shrugged and looked around. They were marooned, at the mercy of the Shumba. Water sloshed against the tires.

He crouched down, hiding from the Shumba, even from himself. He breathed sickening gasoline fumes while Mom prayed, "O Heavenly Father . . ."

As he listened to her prayer and the beat of rain on the roof, the muscles around his ribs cramping, Evan wondered what James Bond would do in a fix like this. He certainly wouldn't lie down and give up. That was for sure.

James Bond would take off in a fancy spy car. He'd levitate right out of this puddle. Or Bond would go back and, hand to hand, fight off all three Shumba, plus more if they came.

But it was silly to think like that. Evan sat up. James Bond was a movie hero, all fake. His game was something he and Blessing used to play at.

Instead, Evan thought of Mahatma Gandhi and Dr. Martin Luther King Jr. They had no guns, no fancy spy equipment. They fought with only their hearts—soul force, the Reverend King called it. No matter how hard things got—even if whole governments were against them—they weren't quitters.

The storm and the car and God had conspired to keep him here for a reason. It was up to him to prevent another riot.

Before Mom could stop him, Evan rolled down the window, climbed out, and leaped into the red water.

A Blinding Curtain

Blessing picked up Evan's fallen bike and hurled it across the grass. He ran to it and threw it again.

The rain came once more in a blinding curtain that almost knocked Blessing to the ground. He ran to the shelter of Mr. Campbell's toolshed. He pounded the workbench with his fist. He pounded again. Jars of nails and screws bounced. He pounded harder, and a hammer fell off the wall.

He caught his breath, put the hammer back on the hook, and sank down.

The rain was light, then heavy. Lightning struck; thunder shook the world.

He should have left Evan to the Shumba. That was what he deserved. After all the years of their being friends, how had it come to this? How could Evan have done what he did and not even have told him?

Blessing pulled up his knees and rested his forehead on them. With a stray nail, he scratched lines on the dusty floor.

Blessing thought back, remembering how Evan had refused to see him when he'd come by with the okra. Did that have to do with Gladman?

Evan had *lied* to him. He'd *deceived* him. Blessing dug at the floor with the nail.

He'd also abandoned him. After the riot, when everyone should have been on the Mission, sorting things out together, standing by one another, praying for the recovery of Caleb and others injured in the riot, Evan had gone off to a white boy's house.

Had he and Evan ever been real friends? Or was he only a toy to Evan, like a tennis racket, a bike, a chess set—just for fun?

Blessing threw the nail across the room.

Dr. Martin Luther King Jr. was surely dreaming to think that Negroes and whites, Africans and whites, could ever *really* be equal.

Hot Water

Evan ran down the road, which flowed like a river, carrying leaves and twigs. He ran across the ankle-deep lake of the churchyard. He dashed down the open hallway of the church, water sloshing from his sandals, and crashed through the door of the reverend's office.

The Reverend Mudavanhu looked up from a book.

Dripping water, Evan said, "Good afternoon, Reverend."

The reverend smiled. "Why, good afternoon, Evan. You're soaked to the skin. What important matter brings you here?"

Evan approached the desk and put both hands on it to steady himself. "Reverend, I have a story to tell. And when I tell it, I need Blessing and three other boys to be here with us."

"Very well," said the reverend. "Sit down."

Just as Evan took a seat, James Zezengwe came in with a tea tray. He set it on the reverend's desk.

"James, please take the umbrella in the corner and run out to get my son, plus . . ." The reverend looked at Evan.

"Petrol, Kingsize, and Lovemore," Evan said. He shook water from his hair.

"Yes, sir," said James, reaching for the black umbrella.

"Here, Evan. Drink some tea." The reverend poured a cup, handed over the little pitcher of milk, and went back to his reading.

Evan added milk to the tea. He sipped it, feeling it slide all the way down, warming his insides.

He sat behind a vase of Gerber daisies, their white petals crisp. He was truly in hot water. He might even get thrown off the Mission. Yet there was nothing left to do but confess everything.

After a few minutes, Petrol came in, slouching, with his arms crossed.

"Please join us, son," the reverend said.

Evan avoided Petrol's stare. He gazed at the last sip of tea: now he didn't dare lift his cup to drink it. He hid behind the daisies.

Blessing arrived next, looking as though he'd run hard. "You didn't leave," he said, panting.

Evan shook his head and smiled at Blessing.

Blessing didn't smile back.

Evan shivered in his soaked clothes.

Lovemore and Kingsize shuffled in together, dripping. They moved their chairs around, scratching the legs against the floor. They thrust sharp looks at Evan.

Blessing scooted close to the reverend's desk.

The Reverend Mudavanhu closed his book. "Boys," he began,

nodding at each of them, "I have called you here because Evan has something to tell us."

Taking a bottle cap from his pocket, Kingsize tossed it from hand to hand.

Evan shivered again. He tried to catch Blessing's eye, but Blessing looked away.

While Kingsize played with the bottle cap, Petrol and Lovemore sat like statues.

"Please start from the beginning, Evan." The reverend patted a pile of books.

When Evan opened his mouth, no words came out.

"Don't be afraid," the reverend whispered.

Evan looked down at his soggy khaki shorts, at his pale hands, folded together, then slowly began: "I found a handbill at the press. It'd fallen down behind the paper cutter." He paused, screwed up his face, looked up, and went on. "It was a handbill showing an African soldier with a gun."

Petrol, Kingsize, and Lovemore glanced at one another.

Blessing leaned forward, his upright wooden chair squeaking.

The reverend twisted the gold band on his finger. "Go on, son," he said.

"I spied at the press. I wanted to see who'd printed that handbill."

"And did you find out?" the reverend asked.

"Yes, sir. Late at night, I saw Gladman running the press. I saw the same peacock-blue paper."

"*Gladman Chinyanga* was printing terrorist literature on the Mission press?" The reverend pushed aside a stack of books.

"Yes, sir."

The rain galloped across the roof.

Blessing's chair squeaked again. Petrol and Kingsize rolled their eyes, and Lovemore slumped with his head in his hands.

Everything went quiet except for the rain.

Evan looked into the lines on his hands, little roads going nowhere.

Softly, the reverend said, "Proceed, son."

"Well, sir, at school, sir, Colonel Rollins told us cadets that it was important to stop Communists."

Suddenly, Blessing stood up, towering over Evan. "You're a *cadet*?"

"A cadet?" echoed Kingsize.

Evan pushed the daisies a little to the side. He looked Blessing in the eye and nodded.

Lovemore sat up, and Kingsize flipped the bottle cap to him.

"You are? You really are?" Blessing said. "And you didn't tell me?"

"I'm sorry. Really sorry. I was ashamed. I'm going to quit, I promise. I'm going to refuse to be a cadet. That is, if I stay. . . ."

If. The little word hung in the air.

"I didn't want to be . . ." Evan murmured. "There was no way out."

A petal dropped off one of the daisies.

"So, Evan," said the reverend, "as a cadet, you went to this Colonel Rollins with the handbill?"

Evan nodded again, shivering in his wet clothes.

The reverend adjusted the white ring of his pastoral collar.

Like needles, the rain fell on the roof.

Again, Blessing stood up. He pointed his finger at Evan and said, "Because of what you did, there was a riot, Evan Campbell. And Caleb got hurt. That was your fault." He jabbed with his finger.

Evan folded his arms across his chest.

"Slow down, son. Sit down." The reverend put up both hands. "The riot was not really *Evan's* fault. It wasn't *he* who incited it. Evan didn't print the handbill. Gladman is the real sinner."

"But, still . . ." Blessing said.

Evan stared at the reverend. For days, he'd shouldered all the blame.

"Evan shouldn't have taken matters into his own hands," said the reverend. "Some might say he erred in turning an African in to the police. Here on the Mission we have other means of solving problems. And Evan shouldn't have kept the secrets he kept."

The room had grown steamy. The reverend got up to open the window. A breeze blew in, cool and gentle. Evan shivered harder.

The reverend sat back down again and looked at Evan. He looked at the Shumba one by one. He put his left hand on the stack of books, the other on a stack of papers. His lips moved as if he was praying.

Evan also prayed: *Jesus, look down on us . . .*

Then the reverend spoke aloud: "Here on the Mission, we have done our best to create a haven where Africans and whites can live together in a spirit of brotherhood and sisterhood. Harmony is our goal. Lately, sadly, we have had much *dis*harmony."

Petrol moved his chair, the legs whining on the concrete floor.

. . . have mercy on us, for we have sinned. . . .

The reverend took off his glasses, wiped them with his handkerchief, and put them back on. "You Shumba are to blame for following Gladman after you knew that he was leading you into trouble. His decisions were unwise." He paused again, while thunder rumbled off in the distance. "I will give you a choice. You may stay at the Mission and walk the path of peace. Or you may leave the Mission for the outside world. And that world, as you know, is none too kind."

A gust of wind blew a splattering of drops out of the trees, onto the roof.

Kingsize stood up. He put his hands in his pockets and said, "I won't stay here with this *bhunu,* who thinks it's a game to betray Africans."

"Me neither," said Lovemore, standing too. "I'll join the *vakomana.*"

They looked down at Petrol, who was still sitting.

Evan folded his hands together and gripped them tightly.

Petrol started to get up, then settled back in his chair. He crossed his arms again.

Kingsize and Lovemore walked out of the room, slamming the door.

The bottle cap rolled to the floor with a quiet clatter. Evan noticed that it wasn't a cap for an innocent soda bottle but rather for Castle beer.

Everyone grew quiet, listening to the footsteps going down the hallway.

Evan listened to the footsteps, wishing they'd turn back, hoping they'd move on.

When the last footstep had sounded, the reverend said, "So, Petrol, you will be staying? You agree to abide by my terms?"

Petrol uncrossed his arms, bowed his head, and said, "Yes, Reverend. My grandmother has sacrificed for me to be in school. I will stay and study."

The rain slowed, and Evan watched water drip from the eaves.

"Maybe later I'll fight," Petrol added. "When it's time."

"I hope you'll walk in peace, son," said the reverend. Then he turned to Evan. "And as for you . . ."

"I'm sorry," Evan said. "I'm sorry, Reverend. I wanted to fight Communism, but I also wanted that medal. Next time I'll think more carefully before I act."

The reverend touched his white collar. "Is that a promise, Evan?"

"Yes, sir." Evan put a hand on his heart.

As the reverend smiled the first smile of the serious meeting, a patch of blue appeared outside the window.

Evan breathed the fresh air coming from the window. Something loosened within him: he was being forgiven. He let the reverend's forgiveness sink into him. It sank slowly, like rain going into the ground.

An idea was forming itself.

Evan reached into his pocket, then placed the cadet medal on the reverend's desk.

The reverend picked up the star-shaped pin.

"What's that?" Blessing asked.

"My cadet medal," Evan said. "I got it for turning in Gladman."

The reverend set the star on the edge of his desk.

Blessing leaned closer. He put out his hand, then drew it back.

Outside, a crow cawed, and another answered.

"Somehow, I'll find a way not to be a cadet," Evan said. "No matter what, I won't be one."

"You won't?" Blessing asked.

"Nobody can make me. My dad didn't fight in the war. I don't have to either."

For the first time, Blessing met Evan's look.

The crows cawed again. It was time to bring forth the idea.

"The Mission needs to be fixed," Evan said, his voice sailing out high but clear. "Since the damage is partly my fault, could I help?" Forming a work party wasn't the kind of thing James Bond would have thought of, but it was the right thing to do. "Mr. Gainsby could show me how."

"But he's leaving," Blessing said. "He and Mrs. Gainsby are leaving."

"Not yet," the reverend said quickly. "Maybe they could be persuaded to stay."

The patch of blue widened. The forgiveness sank deeper.

"How about you, Petrol?" the reverend asked. "Windows all over the Mission have to be replaced. Could you learn to do that?"

Petrol kept his head down but nodded.

"And you, Blessing? Would you like to help?"

Blessing looked at the reverend, then at Evan. He gave a little nod.

And Evan knew then that he'd stay on the Mission. And that Blessing too would forgive him. They'd build that raft, after all.

Sahwira

Blessing sat on the vinyl car seat, sorting okra into bags.

It was the first day of freedom from the work parties. As he worked, Blessing relived those six Saturdays: Mr. Gainsby had taught everyone how to clean out broken windows, how to measure and cut glass, and how to glaze the panes. They'd all worked together, and even Petrol had been friendly.

Rumor had it that Lovemore and Kingsize had crossed the border to join Gladman and the boys in the bush. Blessing imagined them living like leopards, prowling and hunting. One day the three might return. Anytime, they could come with a band of boys to search for Evan.

He and Evan had talked many times about what had happened. Finally, they'd conducted a ceremony—pricking their thumbs and mixing their blood to become blood brothers. They'd vowed that nothing would ever come between them again.

Blessing threw a handful of fluted okra pods into a bag and took up the guitar from the seat beside him.

As he began to pluck the tune to "I Saw Her Standing There," Evan strode into the yard.

"Howdy, John Lennon," his friend called. "Cool guitar. Is that the one you made?"

"Sure is." Blessing held the guitar close. Even Evan didn't have an instrument like this one.

"Looks nice." Evan leaned over and touched the smooth body with his fingertip. "Maybe you'll let me play it someday." He straightened up, saying, "I've got a saw to cut bamboo." He raised the tool so fast the air whistled in the metal teeth.

Blessing laid the guitar carefully on the seat. "I have something even better than that." He went to the shed and returned with an African ax. "This is a *demo.* It'll cut bamboo faster."

Evan took the *demo* and ran his fingertip along the keen edge. He whistled.

"I've been thinking about the raft," Blessing said. "Instead of using nails, we can tie the bamboo together with *msasa*-tree bark. That won't rust."

"Good idea. It'll be like African rope. And we won't have to make holes," Evan said. "No cracked bamboo."

"And this time we'll call the raft the *African King,*" Blessing said. "After the Reverend King."

Evan laughed. "Named for Martin Luther King, it'll float for sure," he said.

"For sure," said Blessing, putting his hands on his hips.

Blessing led the way down the narrow path through a huge green field. With the sun behind them, they walked into their shadows. The blood-red soil and green leaves smelled sweet.

Beyond, the pale-blue sky met the dark-blue mountains.

When they reached the fork in the path, they paused.

Evan reached into his pocket. "Here." He laid the smooth disk of the compass in Blessing's hand. "It's yours now."

"Maiwe!" whispered Blessing.

Evan shifted from one foot to the other. *"Sahwira,"* he added.

"Maiwe, sahwira!" Blessing repeated, smiling. "I had a dream. . . ."

Evan laughed.

When the sun was halfway to high noon, they crossed a stream slipping along a crease in the land.

On the opposite bank, bamboo grew in giant clumps. Blessing gazed up at the straight green poles, the leafy tops tapering into the blue sky. *"Maiwe!"* he said. "It's good bamboo."

"Maiwe!" Evan echoed. "It's a perfect dream." He lifted the African *demo* in salute.

Authors' Note

In 1964, when this fictional story takes place, Rhodesia was between the two big *chimurenga*s, or liberation wars. In the first *chimurenga* (1896–1897), the Africans tried to drive the newly settled white Europeans from their country. The attempt was unsuccessful: the white settlers prevailed.

In the years leading up to the second *chimurenga,* the African continent underwent political transformation. Countries that had been under white colonial rule became independent states governed by Africans. After the countries of Kenya, the Congo, Zambia, Malawi, and Mozambique became self-governing, Rhodesia was the final holdout.

Many in the white Rhodesian government believed that the country could remain under white rule indefinitely. The government portrayed the unrest in Rhodesia as terrorist activity stirred up not by Africans themselves but by Communist agitators from China and the Soviet Union. Rhodesia had, as Prime Minister Ian Smith put it, "the happiest Africans in the world." The government tried to keep the public calm by keeping it largely ignorant.

However, the government's tactics couldn't suppress the uprising. The second *chimurenga* began in 1966 and lasted until 1979. At the end of this struggle, the Rhodesian Africans reclaimed their country. They changed the name from Rhodesia, a word coined from the name of British colonialist Cecil Rhodes, to Zimbabwe, "big house of stone."

The Methodist Church and its missionaries supported social justice and human rights. Pastors and missionaries advocated liberation through peaceful transition instead of armed struggle. The Church fostered education among Africans, sending promising leaders to the United States, England, and India to receive college educations to prepare them to govern the country.

Unfortunately, the liberation achieved in 1979 has not solved Zimbabwe's problems. As of 2008, the country suffers from the highest inflation rate in the world. Simple necessities such as gasoline, health care, electricity, and even adequate food are unaffordable or unavailable for the average African. There is 80 percent unemployment. Those opposing the dictatorship are beaten and abused. Because of political and social unrest, the present period has been referred to by many as the third *chimurenga.*

Glossary

baas Afrikaans: boss

baba Shona: father; also used as a term of respect for a male adult

bhunu Nguni (from the Afrikaans word *Boer*): a derogatory word for white person

bilharzia parasite found in open water in Africa

biscuit British word for cookie

blue-gum trees eucalyptus trees

boobijan Afrikaans: baboon

braivleis Afrikaans: a grill or barbecue

bully beef canned corned beef

chimanje manje Nguni: meaning "now" or "of the present" and used to refer to anything modern such as contemporary music or styles of dress

chimurenga Shona: literally means "struggle"; has come to refer to African liberation wars

Christmas beetles cicadas

dassie Afrikaans: a small mammal resembling a short-eared rabbit

demo Shona: an ax hand made in Rhodesia

el a printer's tool, shaped like the letter *L*

euphorbia a cactus-like plant native to Africa

football soccer

granadilla passion fruit

Iwe, mufana Shona and Nguni: You, child

jelly Jell-O

Jumbo slang for elephant

kaffir derived from Arabic: a derogatory slang term for Africans used by southern African whites; equivalent to the American *N* word

kopje Afrikaans: a small hill; pronounced "KO-pee"

kraal Afrikaans: corral

kudu Hottentot: a kind of antelope with corkscrew horns

lekker Afrikaans: nice or good

lorry British word for truck

mai Shona: mother; also used as a term of respect for a female adult

Maiwe! Shona: Wow! (literally, Oh, you, mother!)

Makadini Shona: How are you?

Mangwanani Shona: Good morning

mapadza Shona: plural form of *badza,* a short-handled hoe

Marmite sandwich spread made of vegetables, the color and consistency of crushed raisins, having a yeasty odor

mbuya Shona: grandmother

mealie corn

mealie-meal cornmeal

mudavanhu Shona: a term of respect, literally "one who loves people"

mufundisi Nguni: teacher

mukoma Shona: friend; a word used between equals

mukwa African mahogany

munt Nguni: a derogatory slang term for Africans used by southern African Europeans

mununʼuna Shona: younger sibling

mupuranga Shona: eucalyptus tree

muriwo Shona: a stew of collard greens, tomato, and onion

mushi Nguni: swell, great

mwanangu Shona: an endearment meaning "my child"

Ndakasimba kana makasimbawo, mai Shona: I am strong (well), if you are strong (well), mother

Ndokurowa! Shona: I'll beat you up!

net ball a game like basketball with no backboard behind the net. The hoop is often made out of a bicycle wheel without the spokes.

Nyama yakanaka! Shona: Good meat!

pastor's manse British term for pastor's home

sadza Shona: a stiff cornmeal porridge

sahwira Shona: a very dear friend who is closer than a relative

Shiri Yekutanga Shona: the First Bird

Shona the native people of Rhodesia; also refers to their language. (Most Shona also speak English, Rhodesia having been a British colony.)

shumba Shona: lion

Smith, Ian prime minister of Rhodesia from 1964 to 1979

stoep Afrikaans: veranda or big porch

tarmac asphalt

terr terrorist

tickey Rhodesian threepence coin

tshombe traitor to the Africans. Moise Tshombe was a political leader in the Congo; it was believed that he was working with Belgian mining companies and white mercenaries, and he was considered a traitor by other African leaders. His name came to be used as a word for "traitor."

tuck shop small grocery store

Unoda kutamba bora here? Shona: Do you want to play ball?

vakomana Shona: literally means "the boys" but came to refer to the freedom fighters in the bush

Varara havo kana mararawo Shona: They slept well if you slept well

Varara here? Shona: How did you sleep?

Zambezi one of the longest rivers in Africa

ZANU Zimbabwe African National Union, an African nationalist party formed in 1963 by Zimbabwean nationalists who were disappointed in the leadership of ZAPU

ZAPU Zimbabwe African People's Union, an African nationalist party formed in 1961. Slogans included "Africa for the Africans," "Majority rule," and "One man, one vote."

Acknowledgments

We would like to acknowledge Tendekayi Muzorewa for his friendship, inspiration, and Shona translation; George Roberts for his encouragement and memories of boarding school in Rhodesia; Jim Kinyon and his brothers for their boyhood projects on the Mission; Ruth Matzigkeit for her personal reminiscence and recollection of the mood of the times; Morgan Johnson for his political cartoons; Morgan and his wife, Rosalie, for their memories of life on the Mission and for helping us maintain the historical accuracy of the text; Kathy (Matzigkeit) Gibb for early critiques; Barbara Matzigkeit for her support; Virginia Loh, Sarah Wones Tomp, and Janice Yuwiler for their weekly critiques; and our editor, Deborah Noyes Wayshak, for her wise and insightful guidance.